Ties That BIND

A Ray Okon Crime Thriller

STANLEY UMEZULIKE

First Published in Great Britain in 2021 by
LOVE AFRICA PRESS
103 Reaver House, 12 East Street, Epsom KT17 1HX
www.loveafricapress.com

ISBN: 978-1-914226-04-5
Also available as ebook

DEDICATION

To Victoria Sanford, thank you for believing in me and helping me take a bold step in my writing career.

ACKNOWLEDGEMENTS

My deepest gratitude goes to the Almighty God, to Him be all the glory.

Throughout the writing of this book, I've had a great team cheering me on, offering advice and providing me with the support I needed to keep moving forward.

My special thanks goes to my great friend, Christiana Agboni. Thank you for your invaluable input and support at every step of the process.

Major thanks to my wonderful author friends, Glory Abah, Ugochukwu Ofoegbu, Damilola Akinbola, Trish Madell, and Sadiq Mustapha, who took time out of their busy schedule to beta read this story.

To my mentor, Victoria Sanford, I'm grateful for your encouragement. Thank you for helping me take a bold step in my writing career.

I owe a special thanks to Amaka Azie, Louis Akwaeze, and Empi Baryeh, for their guidance and support.

I owe a huge debt of gratitude to my family. I'm grateful for your support.

I'm grateful to all the members of Prolific Fiction Writers Community. You are the best.

Thanks also to Uchenna Muodebelu, for cheering me on and being my accountability partner.

Finally, my deepest thanks go to my publisher, Love Africa Press. Thank you for helping to make this dream come true. I'm grateful to all those who helped to bring this book to life. Thank you so much.

PROLOGUE

Mararaba, Abuja

Tamina Ajah did not need a seer to tell her that today would be her last day on earth.

She'd made a terrible mistake. She shouldn't have come back.

Heavy footsteps thumped on the concrete, mixing with the clanking of her high heels. The gunmen were close.

The stilettos were a deterrent to swift motion—time to leave them behind.

Heart-pounding, she pumped her arms hard and ducked into a corner. Catching her breath, she glanced over her shoulders.

Three shadows moved in the dark alley towards her.

Oh, God.

She yanked her shoes off and raced forward. A sharp bend appeared on her left, and she took it, hoping it would lead to freedom.

High brick walls loomed ahead, around her—a dead-end.

Shit.

Pulse-racing, she swivelled to go back.

Three looming, menacing shadows blocked her path. She couldn't see their faces, but she knew who they were—the gunmen.

She was trapped. Nowhere to go. Nowhere to hide.

Terror made her body tremble and her muscles tense. She murmured silent prayers for rescue and safety.

Regret knotted Tamina's belly. She should have gone to the authorities and told them everything. Now, it was too late.

The man in the middle—the tallest among them—strode towards her. The gun in his hand caught the faint light.

Whimpering, she arched her back against the wall until she couldn't move further.

The leader pointed his weapon at her, and her breathing ceased.

"I'm...sorry...for...leaving. I wasn't planning to tell the authorities. Please," she pleaded, her voice breaking apart.

The gunman's fierce eyes did not flicker, and he pulled the trigger.

Tamina let out a shrill cry, and everything went black.

CHAPTER ONE

Kubwa, Abuja

The tension in the pink-coloured room was intense.

"I told you I'll think about it." Loretta Olawale sat on the bed in her apartment and tugged the hem of her dress. Her gaze was fixed on the make-up kits and skin lotions placed atop a round table.

"Baby, you can't keep saying this. Your words hurt. You know how much I love you." Ray Okon, her boyfriend, sat on a white plastic chair in front of her, wearing a black jacket on a white polo and blue jeans.

Once upon a time, she had looked forward to his company. Now she wanted the conversation to end so she could go to work.

Ray stared at her with pleading eyes.

She didn't want to look at him. How would she tell him that something was missing in their relationship? The spark was no longer there.

He'd proposed to marry her, which had caught her off-guard.

Where had that come from? Flustered, she'd told him she would think about it.

Still, how would she tell him that the idea of settling down with him and making babies didn't excite her? She was not yet ready for the considerable commitment. She wanted to grow her business.

As a rising designer in Abuja, she needed to assert herself in the cutthroat fashion industry. She had poured all her sweat into growing the business, and her hard work had paid off.

Unfortunately, it meant her relationship with Ray took a back seat. They had been together since her first year at the university, but now, things had changed.

Fair enough, Ray was a nice guy. He didn't seem to have any problems and had always been supportive. He was humble, caring and a gentleman. Exactly what she needed in a man.

Or was it? Recently, there was no fire in her belly whenever thoughts of him entered her mind. Maybe she'd been lying to herself. The doubts were beginning to creep in. She needed some space. But would Ray understand?

"Honey, I love you too," she said, hoping they could work it out. "But right now, I need some space. I don't understand what is going on, either. Just give me a little time to figure it all out."

***

Ray rose from his seat and paced the room.

He could not believe it. Loretta's words were like a punch in his gut.

They had been inseparable right from day one, a match made at the University of Lagos. But right now, it seemed like the walls were falling apart. For over three months, she had seemed distracted. He would call, she wouldn't pick. Worst, she would not return his calls. It drove him crazy.

Ray was a low-level analyst at the Department of State Services at the Abuja Central Branch. For the past two weeks, as he sat behind his desk at work, he couldn't concentrate. He couldn't point out the problem, and the uncertainty in his relationship was giving him panic attacks.

God, he loved her so much. Had always loved her—right from the first day they'd met at the University of Lagos. His friends would always joke that they were lovebirds.

But since he proposed to her two months ago, she had not given him an answer. In fact, it was clear that she had been avoiding him. What did he do wrong? Maybe it was because he didn't have much money.

As a fashion designer, her clients ranged from Abuja big boys to hotshot executives. Did she want Ray to be like those highfliers?

He wasn't, though. Against those men, he felt inadequate in comparison.

What would he do? As he scrambled for a solution, his chest tightened, and an angry headache attacked him.

Ray was already getting frustrated at his job. He had trained and worked for six years in the DSS. He had put in his sweat and given his best, and yet, they had denied him a promotion and the one thing he craved the most— a job as a field agent.

Instead, they'd stuck him at the desk. He loved his country, and he loved working at the agency. He had poured his energy and years of hard work into the job. Didn't he deserve better?

Maybe his lady was seeing him as a total failure.

Since Loretta wouldn't tell him the truth, his mind conjured so many absurd assumptions.

Today, he'd come here to find answers. This Saturday morning, he had called, and she didn't pick, and he decided to visit. He'd asked her what the problem was, and she kept saying words that were slowly breaking his heart.

He paused his pacing and faced her. "Baby, you are not making any sense. Please, talk to me. What is really going on?"

Silence.

Then, she sighed, rose from the bed, and began to undress in front of him. She ignored him, sauntered into the bathroom, leaving him speechless.

She was changing right in front of him. There was no doubt about that.

Ray shook his head and walked out of the house. He climbed onto his motorcycle, fired up the engine and barrelled it down the road.

CHAPTER TWO

DSS Office, Abuja Central Branch

Ray walked past his fellow analysts, greeting a few with a wave of his hand before heading to his cubicle.

The whole first floor was a vast expanse of desks and cubicles. The workspace was quiet except for the sounds of tapping fingers on computer keyboards.

Eleven people occupied the office, each with a desk and computer with a big monitor. Their role was simple: to do the bulk of paperwork and help DSS field agents do their job.

This was why Ray hated this job. He was missing the action out there. He didn't belong here.

He sat on his chair and rested his head to calm his nerves. His personal life was in a mess. Everywhere he looked, it would seem nothing made sense anymore.

One of his nearby colleagues, Christine Zainab, a woman of average height in her early thirties and one of the top analysts in their branch, saw the look of resignation on his face and approached his desk.

"Ray, today is Monday. Why are you looking like your heart was broken during the weekend?" She broke into laughter.

Ray hated her when she did that. Christine loved to make expensive jokes, but this time, she was right even though she didn't know it yet.

He had been fighting a losing battle to push Loretta out of his mind, but Christine's words made all the memories come rushing back. Within a minute, his mind went back in time to the very moment when he met Loretta for the first time.

***

The day was Saturday. August's rainy season was in full effect, with a heavy downpour rushing every few minutes. The sky was angry and had succeeded in chasing the sun away.

It was the day for the entrance examination into the University of Lagos. The nineteen-year-old Ray was dressed in a pressed white shirt and black trousers. The shirt was tucked in and neat.

He sat inside a cab, hoping to make it for the nine o'clock exam. When the driver passed the massive school gate, he saw her.

She looked frantic in rain-soaked clothes and teary eyes.

He peered out through the car window, their eyes met, and his heart melted.

"Driver, please stop. Park close to the gate," he ordered.

The driver did as he told him, and Ray alighted from the car and rushed to where she stood.

"Hi, what happened? Are you among those that will be taking the exam today?" he asked.

"Yes, a motorcycle rider dropped me here, and since then, I've not seen a taxi that will take me inside the campus to the venue of the exam. My exam is by nine this morning, and right now, it's ten minutes to nine. I'm new in this town, and I don't know anyone here." Her voice was halting and panicky.

Her worry was written all over her face.

"It's okay. I'm also writing the same examination as well. The venue is DLI. I have a taxi, and I'm heading there now. Please, join me, let's go. The rain is getting too much."

A smile spread across her face.

"Thank you so much. You are a lifesaver." Her voice had an emotional edge to it.

They sprinted towards the cab and got in.

Ray gave her the new white handkerchief he'd bought earlier that morning. "Use this to wipe your face. Take a deep breath. You will be fine."

She collected it from him and said, "Thank you."

The driver restarted the engine and drove across a long winding road, passing beautiful shrubs, flowers, and newly built lecture halls. Both Ray and the girl peeped through the car window with wonder in their eyes.

This was the prestigious University of Lagos. They were so close to clinching their dreams.

When they reached a bend, the driver took a left, drove past Forte Oil, and kept going down the straight road until he stopped in front of their exam venue. A signpost displayed—Distance Learning Institute E-Resource Centre, popularly known on the campus as DLI—in bold red letters was mounted close to the yellow building.

Students poured in and out of the building, most of them carrying documents they would use for the exam.

Ray and the girl climbed down from the vehicle.

Ray paid the cab driver, and they sprinted towards the building. The heavy downpour reduced to a drizzle.

Both wrote the computer-based test.

When Ray came out of the examination hall an hour later, he'd forgotten about the stranger. His mind was focused on what they asked him for the Criminal Law course he applied for. Did he get question fourteen correct? He would check when he got back to his house.

"Hi," a female voice interrupted his thoughts.

He looked into the bright eyes of a young girl with the most adorable smile, spotless brown skin, and braided hair arranged neatly in a ponytail.

"Hi," he said, and recognition set in. It was the girl he helped get to the exam venue.

"We meet again. How was your exam?" she asked.

"It went smoothly. How about yours?"

"It was amazing. Thank you for your act of kindness. Without your help, I wouldn't—"

Ray raised his hand.

"Don't mention it. I did nothing special. I wish us both successes in the exams. Have a nice day," he said and flashed her a warm smile. "I have to run. See you later."

He strode towards the road and raised his hand to hail a taxi.

"Wait."

Her voice made him stop. He glanced back and saw her staring at him with pleading eyes.

"You didn't tell me your name." She raised her voice so he could hear her above the chatter of the noisy crowd of young people gathered at the gate after taking their exams.

"My name is Ray Okon."

She approached him and said, "My name is Loretta Olawale. It's nice meeting you."

Ray smiled. "It's nice meeting you as well."

"Let's share contacts so we can congratulate each other when the results come out," she suggested.

"That will be a good idea." And they did.

Three weeks after that, their results came out, and they congratulated each other. Then the admission was released. Loretta got admitted into Textiles and Fashion Design, and Ray got accepted into the Faculty of Law.

She called, and they congratulated each other. That was the beginning of phone calls that blossomed into a deep friendship. During their second year at the university, their relationship took a step further when Ray gave her a surprise kiss on Valentine's day. She returned the favour, and the new lovers enjoyed a wild night of bliss.

Even though Ray was older by two years, both worked as a team and even when storms crossed their paths, nothing could tear them apart.

Ray had an intelligent and analytic mind. Loretta was a natural leader and a young woman with exceptional grace and the ambition to keep pushing herself to achieve her goals. Together, they were like two peas in a pod.

After graduation, Loretta, who used her tailoring skill to survive in the university, pursued her lifelong dream of becoming a fashion designer. Ray, who excelled in Criminal Law, got a job in the country's Department of State Services after training at the State Security Services Academy in Lagos.

Everything had been going great, although their different careers pulled them into diverse worlds. Now, Ray could feel the distance between them.

***

The ringing intercom at his desk jarred Ray from memory.

He picked it.

"Ray." It was the voice of Martin Ajayi, PA to the station chief at their branch office.

"Hello, Martin."

"Chief wants to see you at his office tomorrow morning."

"Time?"

"10 am."

CHAPTER THREE

Garki, Abuja

"Ma'am, the models who will wear the strapless gowns are not ready," Loretta's personal assistant, Jane Nwobodo, said.

"Are the evening wears ready?"

"They will be ready in three days, ma'am."

"Have you contacted the people that invited us to confirm the time for our own show?"

"Not yet, ma'am."

"Then, what are you still doing here?" Loretta glared at the younger woman.

Jane cringed with fear and dashed out of her boss's office.

Loretta clenched her jaw and banged her fist on the table. Since she arrived at her fashion house, her anger had risen through the roof.

A week ago, she finally got her big break to showcase her designs at the upcoming Abuja International fashion week. Now, these brats wanted to spoil everything for her.

She left her office and entered an ample space where five women toiled at electric sewing machines. Pieces of clothing lay scattered everywhere. They saw her, and panic settled on their faces. She glanced at them one last time and strode into a room beside her office.

This was her design space—a small room wallpapered with pictures of women in fashionable clothes.

There were storyboards, pencils, eraser, pen, needle and wool and a tape and a cardboard paper with sketches. There were pieces of clothing in different shapes and computer-drawn designs.

Loretta's fabrics were her children. She understood how they move, drape, breathe and swing around the body when worn.

Her intimate knowledge of fabrics and her ability to visualise the finished product when looking at mere pencil-drawn sketches set her apart in the industry. She believed she inherited this gift from her late mother, who had been a tailor.

Loretta started tailoring in her university days. It enabled her to survive and made sure she was not solely dependent on her aunt, who paid her school fees. When she graduated, she took the bold step and pursued her dream of becoming a fashion designer.

As a young girl working in her mother's tailor shop, she had admired her mother's designs. She used to go through the fashion magazine her mother bought from time to time. Whenever a customer wanted her to sew an unusual designer wear, her mother would bring out the magazine.

"Look at these designs and choose the one you like," she used to say in her soft voice Loretta loved so much. They would choose, and the young Loretta would watch, fascinated as her mum transformed small pieces of fabrics into beautiful clothing. Her customers kept coming back.

As Loretta grew, designers such as Nigeria's Deola Sagoe and Folake Folarin Coker—creative director of Tiffany Amber fashion brand, became her role models in the industry.

During her National Youth Service—when fresh graduates served their country for one year after graduation—she did a six-month advanced fashion design course. She was taught drawing, colour and composition, pattern making and draping.

A year after that, she worked as an intern at the famous House of Vanessa—a big fashion house in Abuja.

She stayed for one year and learned first-hand from one of the most successful fashion designers in the industry. There, she also understood the business side of the craft.

Her specialities were ready-to-wear dresses and evening wear for women. Today, she was happy she decided to follow this path.

Already, she was doing well. She had been able to build a relationship with top celebrities in the country.

Last year, she designed a red gown adorned with sapphires, worn by a female Big Brother Nigeria Finalist at the African Magic Viewers' Choice Awards.

To Loretta's delight, the superstar, Vivian Peters, was given the award as the best-dressed female. As the dress began to trend on Social Media, her fans began to search for the designer.

Within forty-eight hours, Loretta's Instagram followers—which she saw as her 'prospective clients' grew from 1000 to 10,000. Since then, she'd been on a winning streak, building more connections and gaining the leverage she needed in the industry. Vivian paved the way for her to be invited to this year's Abuja International Fashion Week. The event would be coming up in a few days, and she would not let anything go wrong.

She spent the rest of the day working on an attire for a Nollywood actress. By five in the evening, her phone beeped. She picked it and opened the message.

"Babe, I'm coming to your house this evening. I have good news," the message read.

Typical Cynthia.

Just as well. She was exhausted and packing up for the day. She dropped some instructions for Jane and took a taxi that would take her home.

***

Kubwa, Abuja

"Babe, I'm getting married," Cynthia Okeke said to her best friend, Loretta, as she showed her the diamond ring.

Both were on the sofa in Loretta's living room drinking juice and watching 'Keeping Up with the Kardashians.'

Her news made Loretta sit upright. Slowly, a smile warmed up her face. "When did Chuks propose?"

"This afternoon. He didn't even tell me he was going to propose. He took me to ShopRite, knelt and did it in front of all the people there. You know how I hate that. Geez, I was so shy. I wanted to..." Cynthia kept babbling about how she felt when her man surprised her.

Cynthia had the hourglass figure of a beauty queen. Her dark-brown skin complemented her blue spaghetti-strap dress. Cynthia always chose the sophisticated over the simple.

They had been best of friends since their University days when Cynthia had been her gist partner. She'd known all the gossip floating around the campus. Destiny kept bringing them together.

Loretta listened as Cynthia kept gushing about her fiancée, Chuks, and the diamond engagement ring he gave to her. Loretta wondered why Cynthia didn't toe the path of fashion design. Instead, she went down the medical way and worked as a nurse in a government hospital.

During their University days, Cynthia was the fashion queen and became Miss Nursing in their third year. She then met Chuks, who'd been the Student Union President, and both started dating. Now they were getting ready to tie the knots. Loretta's eyes glistened with tears. She looked away and wiped her tears. When she looked back to face her friend, she had transformed into a smiling princess.

"Loretta, you are not listening!"

Loretta heard the voice and snapped back to reality. "What did you say?"

"Will you please accept? Please." Cynthia's voice was pleading.

Loretta's eyes narrowed. "What?"

"Will you be my chief bridesmaid?"

Loretta heard her and swallowed hard. Typical Cynthia, the life of the party. She flashed a forced smile. "Of course, babe. If I'm not the one, who will? I accept."

"Really?" Cynthia exclaimed like a child whose mum had finally said yes to her request. She drew Loretta close and hugged her tight. At that moment, the phone she held in her hand rang. She answered the call.

"Honey, what are you waiting for?" the voice at the other end of the line said.

"Oh, sweetheart, I'm on my way," she said and hung up.

"Cynthia, what is it?" Loretta asked as she observed her friend.

"It's a call from my fiancé. We planned to meet this evening. Babe, I gotta go. I will call you." She gave Loretta a peck on both cheeks and dashed out of the house, leaving Loretta wondering about what just happened.

Cynthia carried a tremendous amount of energy with her, and once she left, it was as though she took all of it with her. She had stopped calling her man Chuks. Now, she preferred to address him with his new title, 'Fiancé.'

Was her friend brandishing that in her face?

Loretta tapped her feet on the floor. Her body was getting hot as doubts she had about her relationship and uncertain future surged through her.

What would she do about Ray? She banished the thought from her mind. She had a more significant priority, and it wasn't to worry about men or a lack of men in her life. Now was time for her to focus on growing her business.

***

The next day, Loretta was in her office, but she couldn't concentrate. Thoughts about her relationship with Ray plagued her mind.

One of Loretta's fears was that she didn't want to end up like her mother.

Her parents had enjoyed the early years of their marriage. Her father, Cyril Olawale, was a Nigerian businessman in Jamaica. There he met his heartthrob, the beautiful Campbell, a tailor in a shop close to a restaurant frequented by tourists. Both clicked instantly and married in the Island Nation. Campbell, the Jamaican woman, was willing to do anything for love. She travelled with her husband to his country, Nigeria.

In the third year of their marriage, the couple gave birth to Loretta. They devoted their time to raising their daughter. Her father loved her so much and named her Adewale. Two years later, their dream fell apart, and everything changed.

Cyril was deceived in a business deal by his father-in-law, who was also his business partner. The business crumbled, and Campbell, who wasn't talking to her family, hated her father the more. She moved to Nigeria with her husband and their child. But few years in, Cyril tried several times to snatch a comeback and rebuild his business but failed.

The family had to depend on Campbell, who kept things afloat with the meagre income from her tailoring business. But it wasn't enough. As the months turned into years, the couple began to quarrel due to money problems, and the love faded away.

Cyril turned to women and booze for temporary pleasure. When he returned home and faced accusation from his wife, she would bear the brunt of his frustration.

As Loretta grew, her father stopped bringing money home. No one knew what he did. The little income he made during the day, he'd spend them on his mistresses.

Soon, the home was no longer a place of refuge for the young Loretta. She would often spend time with Doris, who started training her when she entered high school.

Three months later, her parents had one of their quarrels. This time, it was fierce and violent, the house strewn with broken chairs and tables.

The next day, her father ran away with one of his mistresses, and her mother suffered a mild heart attack and was rushed to the hospital.

Loretta never heard from him after that.

For many years, her mother was in and out of hospitals. Her health went from bad to worse. For over six months, during Loretta's twenty-first year, her mother was in the hospital, surrounded by nurses in blue tunics, a beeping monitor displaying her heart rate and drips attached to her weak veins.

She remembered the way her mother looked at her from her sickbed, her face tight and weary. As Loretta watched her mother, she didn't know when she broke down in tears. Her mother had aged by ten years. Her face looked dull, and sadness wound tight around her eyes.

Her mother took her hand in her weak hands and said, "My daughter, your marriage won't be like mine. You will marry a man who will treat you right. Now wipe your tears and smile for mama."

Her mother's voice grew faint each minute.

Loretta replied with a nod and forced a smile. She stayed with her mother throughout the night. The next day, her mother's heart stopped beating, and the twenty-one-year-old Loretta wept like a baby. No one could console her.

Loretta's childhood experience affected how she viewed relationships.

On the surface, she was a confident, driven woman but deep within her, she feared she would marry a man like her father.

Although she had feelings for Ray, she had not fully opened her heart to him or any man. The walls were still there, around her heart. They took years to build.

Sometimes, she would feel so ashamed to be with Ray. He'd been her first love.

Now her heart said she'd been lying to herself, and Ray was not the man for her.

Yet, what else was she looking for in a man? The doubts refused to go away.

"Ma'am, it's time for the meeting," Jane's voice brought her back from her reverie.

Loretta snapped back into focus and sat ramrod straight on the executive chair. The Apple laptop on her desk alerted her to a new email message. She clicked on it and perused the content.

The Abuja International fashion week's organisers had sent a message to all the fashion designers who would participate in the event. They were officially notifying her about the date and the time for her own models to display her designs.

She noted the vital information and replied to the message, sending her gratitude. When she raised her head, her personal assistant was still in her office.

"Thank you, Jane. I'll be there in five minutes," she said and waved her off.

Jane nodded and left.

Loretta rose and took two files from the desk. She had a meeting with her staff to go through plans for the fashion week, which would begin in four days.

CHAPTER FOUR

DSS Office, Abuja Central Branch

Today was the long-awaited day—time for another performance review.

This morning, as Ray had showered, dressed, and arrived at the office, he'd resisted the temptation to check his phone or email for new messages. He didn't want to ask his co-workers either. He was afraid he would be passed over *again*.

Anxiety knotted his gut, and his feet were unsteady as he did the long walk to his boss's office.

The personal assistant to the station head sat at the front desk. In his early thirties, he was dark-skinned and dressed in a white shirt and black trousers.

"Hi, Martin," Ray said, injecting confidence into his tone.

Martin looked up from his computer before speaking into the intercom. He lowered the phone and said, "Hi Ray, please enter. He is ready for you."

"Thank you, Martin."

Ray pushed the huge door and entered the office of DSS Abuja-Central Station Chief.

The office was gold-carpeted and unusually large. The boss, Ezekiel Bassey, a grey-haired man in his late fifties, sat on a black leather chair behind a mahogany desk. Two visitors' seats faced his desk. Two adjacent black leather sofas occupied the centre of the room. A massive shelf with books and file stacks spanned the length of the right-hand wall.

Mr Bassey was reading a report from a manila folder. A laptop with a big screen sat atop his desk. He stared at the big screen and resumed his reading.

Ray closed the door.

His boss stopped reading and motioned with his right hand. "Please, get settled on the sofa."

Ray nodded and sat on one of the sofas, feet tapping on the floor. His anxiety made the office atmosphere seem tense.

Seeking guidance, he glanced at his boss and understood why people said Mr Bassey was difficult to read.

The man's expression was blank.

Hopefully, the man would break the bad news quickly so Ray could be out of here and back to his desk.

The station chief was known to be a principled man. He'd arrived three years earlier and cleaned house, his intention to only work with the best. Whenever he came to work in the morning, he'd offer a ready smile, nothing else.

Still, it wasn't difficult to understand his aloofness. A man with no wife, no kids—according to official records—was married to the agency.

Ray's heart thumped erratically.

He'd expected to sit at one of the chairs at the desk. Instead, his boss joined him, settling on the second sofa with a grin on his face.

"Good morning, sir," Ray said.

"Good morning, Ray." Mr Bassey replied. "Let me go straight to the point. I know you must wonder why I called you here."

Ray nodded. The smiling man unnerved him. Was he about to be sacked?

"Ray Okon, you've worked with the agency for six years, and you've been dedicated to your duty," the man continued.

"When I took this job three years ago, I reviewed your file. Your training scores and achievements astounded me, and I thought you were in the wrong position. We were wasting our best talents. So, I've been sending letters to the Directory General who promised to do something about it."

Mr Bassey glanced at the file in his hand. "Now he's placed you where the agency can best harness your skills. First, I must apologise on behalf of the agency for the delay due to bureaucratic red tape."

Ray narrowed his eyes. Where was this going?

"Finally, the agency has responded. Better late than never, right? They looked at your file and my own recommendation and sent a positive response. This is in line with my goal of leading a high-performing team. You can't tell a fish to fly, but it would do it better than a bird if you tell it to swim. Congratulations, Ray, you've been promoted to DSS Field Agent." Mr Bassey extended his hand.

Everything moved fast. Ray's analytical brain seemed slow to comprehend. He extended his hand and took his boss's in a firm handshake.

"This is not the main reason I called you here," his boss continued. "With the new promotion comes bigger responsibility. You've been reassigned to Homicide and Anti-Drug Trafficking Unit. Your new position means you'll get an official car and a monthly wardrobe allowance. Thank you for your professionalism and fierce determination to your job over the years. You will work with Breya and Frank on an important investigation."

Mr Bassey rose from his seat, strode to his desk, and returned with a big khaki-coloured envelope. "This envelope includes the car key, details about your promotion and the case file."

"Thank you, sir, I don't know what to say. I didn't expect this," Ray said as he accepted the file.

His pulse rate accelerated, and relief flushed through him. He regained inner confidence, and for the first time in a long while, his body surged with excitement. All the years of hard work had finally paid off.

"The last three years, HATU has been working on an important case involving dangerous criminals who have been terrorising our city. Since then, they have made little headway. They lack your analytical skills—" he tilted his head "—exactly why you're needed. Plus, there has been a major development. Classified information you weren't aware of since you don't have security clearance. After you've been processed, Breya, the team leader, will brief you on everything you need to know about the case."

"Thank you, sir, for having confidence in me. I promise to do my best."

"I know you will, Agent Ray."

Ray went back to his cubicle afterwards. At noon, a senior DSS officer helped him process his verification and security clearance. He was given two additional files, which he put inside the envelope.

He stayed in his cubicle until four in the evening. Some of his colleagues had already gone home. As he finished clearing his desk, his phone beeped.

He brought it out from his trouser pocket and read the message from Loretta.

"I want to see you. We have something important to discuss."

Ray wondered what was up as he grabbed the envelope and strode out of the building.

CHAPTER FIVE

Kubwa, Abuja

By the time Ray reached Loretta's apartment, the sky had transformed into a deep orange.

A gentle breeze caressed his face as he climbed out of his motorcycle, still clutching his envelope. In good spirits, he whistled a tune and ambled to the door.

With a knock, he entered and halted in surprise.

Loretta stood, hands akimbo, in her living room, like she'd been waiting for him.

"Honey, I got your message. What happened?"

She avoided his gaze. "I've thought about your proposal and made a decision. That was why I called you."

"Go on."

"If you are ready for marriage, I won't delay you. I'm grateful for the support you have given me over the years, and I'm sorry to say this. But, right now, I want to focus on growing my business. I don't have space in my life for marriage."

He hadn't just heard her right. This was not Loretta. His Loretta.

Ray took a step forward, but his eyes widened as she moved back. "Honey, what are you saying?"

Loretta quickly raised her hand. "Please don't. Look at your job. For many years now, they keep passing you over when it's time for a promotion. Don't you think you deserve better? I don't want any man in my life right now, but even if I do, I'd want my man to be bold enough to fight for his rights."

"Honey, you don't understand. You haven't allowed me to talk to you. I have some good news to—"

She quickly raised her voice over his. "Spare me the crap, please. This is what you have been telling me over the years. I don't need any of it. You're lagging in office politics. I advise you to get your act together in that regard. But that's not the reason why I am doing this. I'm not ready. I just want to focus on my business. My heart does not have space for any man in my life right now."

Ray couldn't stay still. He paced across the room. "So, this is it? Are you breaking up with me?"

She quickly replied. "Yes, Ray. I want you to forget about me and move on. I want you to..."

He stopped listening. Old memories rushed back and took his mind to another place and time.

***

They were celebrating her twentieth birthday during their third year at the university.

After the birthday party, they took a slow, leisurely walk to the famous love garden on the campus. It was nine in the evening, and the blue moon bathed the well-groomed garden making the place a perfect location for young lovers.

Every few minutes, both would burst into laughter. They didn't want to observe other couples in the vast, circular garden. It was just the two of them in the world. Nothing else mattered.

They sat on benches, facing each other, licking ice cream. Afterwards, they held hands and watched the shade of the moon deepen.

"Honey, after graduation, what do you want out of life?" Ray asked.

Loretta's face beamed so brightly. "You, and a successful career in fashion design." Her voice was like music to his ears.

His breathing became erratic, and he leaned forward, crushing his lips on hers. She tasted of ice cream and Loretta.

* * *

In their final years and examination fast approaching, tragedy struck.

Ray was aware of Loretta's family issues—an absconded father and an ill mother. He'd visited her sick mother several times.

On the fateful week, he'd travelled out of school. On his return, he called her.

Loretta showed at his off-campus dwelling minutes later, crying.

He'd held her in his arms, tears streaming down his face as she recounted the tragic moments when her mother passed away.

"I watched her die," she said through sobs. "I can't sleep. I can't study. I'm so scared. I don't know what else to do. Can I stay with you tonight, please?"

"Of course, sweetheart," he said and held her tight.

That night, she woke every few minutes, tormented by unseen enemies and nightmares, but Ray was right there by her side.

* * *

Two and a half years later, she finished her internship and started her own business.

Ray was in State Security Services Academy in Lagos when she called. "Honey, the fashion industry is a jungle. It's like kill or be killed. It's merciless, and the competition is killing me. I'm not sure I'm cut out for this."

Ray quickly said, "Sweetheart, this is your passion, remember. You're ready for this. You will thrive. Don't let anyone tell you otherwise. All those experienced fashion designers you admire were once like you. You are doing great, and I am so proud of you."

"Thank you so much, Darling. I needed this so much. This is why I will always love you."
***

The memories played until her words *'This is why I will always love you'* made him snap back to reality.

What about all the promises? Did they mean nothing to her?

He took a deep breath and calmed the tension ravaging his body.

She faced him, waiting to hear what he had to say. Or maybe she wanted to see him break down.

But Ray was not a man who was used to showing his emotions. He'd heard her message loud and clear, and he had nothing more to say to her. He wouldn't be an obstacle to her path to success—if that was how she wanted to put it.

A man of few words, he believed his presence was no longer needed here. What was he still doing here anyway?

There was no need for him to share the good news with her. She didn't want him in her life anymore, and it pained him that he had to accept the truth that was staring him in the face.

The living room suddenly felt like it was suffocating him. Beads of sweat appeared on his forehead.

With his envelope still in hand, he nodded at her and carried his five-feet-ten frame out of the house. Then he climbed his motorcycle, and the engine soon kicked back to life.

Within seconds, he was out of the premises and out of her life.
***

Loretta refused to wipe the tears forming at the corners of her eyes as she watched Ray leave her apartment.

Had she been too harsh on him?

They'd been inseparable for years. Now, she'd ended it all.

Had she done the right thing?

Truthfully, she was scared. Her life was changing fast.

She'd had to make the difficult decision. This was the price she had to pay at this point in her journey for success.

It wouldn't be easy to go far in the industry, so she had to commit herself and not allow any distractions.

Yesterday, she had an important meeting with her staff. They finalised plans for the Abuja Fashion Week starting in three days. This was the big break she needed to focus on.

Not relationships. Or marriage.

Ray was a wonderful guy. He'd been good to her.

But she couldn't give him what he wanted. Her family history meant her heart was closed to any man.

She locked the door and turned to go back to her kitchen and prepare her dinner. But as she turned, a tear dropped onto her cheek.

CHAPTER SIX

DSS Abuja Central Branch
The following day, Ray walked into the DSS briefing room located on the building's second floor. Earlier, he'd gotten a text message that he and his new team had a briefing by nine.

Ray was dressed in his black-on-black DSS uniform. He met with Breya Adams, the team leader. Breya was a heavily-built man in his late thirties. While Ray was dark, lean, and athletic, Breya was chocolate and had Dwayne Johnson's body. His black beard was huge, but he looked the part of a typical DSS agent.

Ray greeted Frank Igwe next. Frank was a man in his early forties. Average height, plain-looking, solid on the ground and particularly good with a weapon. Frank also worked as a liaison with the police. Their chief, Ezekiel Bassey, joined them ten minutes later.

The briefing room's front wall was covered with big screens that the agency used for teleconferencing and daily briefings.

"Welcome, Agent Ray. We are glad you are here with us," Breya said.

Frank came forward and shook hands with him.

"Thank you, guys," Ray said.

"Breya, what's the latest update on the case? Bring us up to speed," Ezekiel said.

Breya pointed the remote at the wall of screens, and a face covered with a question mark appeared on a monitor. He pressed the remote the second time, and pictures of young women huddled together appeared. Next was a picture of recovered guns and contraband drugs.

"Three years ago, the city of Abuja was flooded with illicit drugs. In fact, no one knew what was going on until young men and women started turning up on the roadside, with alcohol and drugs in their system. A few months later, a series of road crashes increased in the city, and we lost so many youths to these crashes. When autopsies were done, we detected tramadol and cocaine in their system."

"That was just the beginning," Frank added.

"Yes, it became worse. We turned undercover and started going to nightclubs, bars, and motels. That was when we discovered what was really going on. The city had changed, and this took everyone, including the law enforcement agencies, by surprise. We discovered that the nightclubs, bars, and motels were flooded with these illicit drugs—mostly cocaine, heroin, and codeine. Our young men and women were consuming them. We also discovered a surge of tramadol—an opioid painkiller legally and legitimately prescribed by doctors for pain relief—in the streets. Our youths, especially those living in Abuja slums, take these pills in life-threatening doses as a stress reliever and a cheaper way to get high and forget about their suffering. The next thing we did was to find out how these drugs were entering the country."

Ray watched the screen as he listened.

"Since then, we've made tremendous progress. Today, we know that these are just the tip of the iceberg."

"What do you mean by that?" Ray asked.

"We are dealing with a dangerous criminal cartel. They are heartless men that deal in the smuggling of illicit drugs and human trafficking. They also control prostitution rings in Italy and Dubai, luring young, innocent girls to these countries with the promise of a better life."

"Who are these people?" Ray asked.

"Good question. That's the problem," said Breya. He pointed the remote at the screen again and a face covered with question mark dominated the screens. "We still don't know who they are. But from the Intel we've gotten so far from their victims who talked, we believe that this cartel is controlled by a drug lord in his mid-forties, and they operate out of Italy and Dubai. The members of this cartel are professionals and have been able to evade law enforcement agencies for the past three years."

"They are turning our young people into zombies with all these hard drugs. This has become an embarrassing crisis that has reached the desk of the president," Ezekiel said.

"We have made arrests, but we still don't know what we are dealing with. We've discovered that most of the people we arrested are pimps, drug users, and decoys who were just the victims," Frank said.

Breya pointed the remote at the wall again, and a picture of a young woman appeared on the screen. "Recently, there has been a major development in this case. This is Tamina Ajah. She was in her early thirties. Her body was found inside a gutter at Mararaba Junction three days ago. Initial investigation revealed that she was murdered."

Ray and the rest of the people in the room looked up as Breya displayed more graphic images of the dead woman. The last picture revealed a hole in her head. Ray gasped.

"Autopsy reports showed that there was a high dosage of cocaine in her system. Tamina was last seen two weeks ago at a hotel in Dubai where she worked as a call girl."

"So, they brought her down to Nigeria and killed her? It doesn't make sense," Ray said, his brain already looking for answers.

"That's what we presume at this moment," said Breya. "We know how these men operate. They are ruthless. They lure these girls to Italy and Dubai with a promise of a better life and force them to work as sex workers in those brothels. If they ever disobey an order, they are disposed of at once."

Everyone kept quiet for a while, and the tension in the room increased.

"Ray, what's your take on this? What do you think happened here?" Ezekiel asked.

Ray studied the picture on the screen for a long moment. And then a thought entered his mind. "There is a question no one has answered yet. What if they also have a prostitution ring right here in Abuja, under our noses?"

"Impossible," Breya interjected. "They can't take such a risk."

Ray looked at his boss and said, "Sir, I have just one request to make."

"Please, go on."

"I would like to see the body."

"Breya, make it happen tomorrow."

"Yes, sir," Breya replied.

"I want this case to be wrapped up as soon as possible. You guys will be given everything you need. I'll coordinate with headquarters to make this happen. You have orders to find and arrest these criminals and bring them in to face the wrath of the law," Ezekiel said.

"Yes, sir," everyone said in unison.

"Breya, I want daily updates on this case."

"Yes, sir."

Ezekiel left the room, and soon afterwards, the rest of the team dispersed. After the briefing, Ray drove his new Camry to his two-bedroom apartment at Wuse, with just the basics. He converted his bedroom to his makeshift office, where he usually poured through pages of documents at night. The guest bedroom was for visitors. In the living room, a flat-screen TV set hung on the wall. Two comfortable couches sat in the middle. He sank on his couch as soon as he entered his living room.

Even though he was exhausted, his face brightened. His mind was already focused on this case, looking at many possibilities, none of which was good news. But he would keep them to himself until he could back it with evidence. He switched on the television and watched as a female news correspondent discussed the gruesome murder of Tamina Ajah.

Ray had been brought in to where he belonged. He relished the pleasure and rush of adrenaline that pumped through him. As he showered five minutes later, his gut instinct told him that this shit not only smelled, but it was also rotten. First, he'd need to see the body.

CHAPTER SEVEN

The morgue was an old building at Maroman road.

Ray, Frank, Breya and John Esie, a light-skinned medical examiner who worked for the agency, had gathered outside its worn-out gate an hour ago. This was a morgue owned by the agency where they ran autopsy on murder victims. They usually gave the family and relatives a time window to identify the corpse and claim it.

Frank approached the gateman, a dark heavyset man in his early seventies. They spoke briefly, and he unlocked the gate. The men entered and advanced across the vast compound. Frank unlocked and opened the front door, and they went in. The wooden floorboard creaked under their weight. They walked with care and soon entered a large room where the corpses were kept.

Ray was the last to enter. His eyes swept across the room, and he hated everything in it—the dust smelt of rusted pipe. The room was dark and filled with cobwebs. They had to open some of the windows to allow the sunlight to stream in.

John led them to the place where the corpse was kept. Hers was the only corpse in the room. The corpse was covered from head to toe with a white sheet. John uncovered the head, and someone in the group gasped as they stared at the dead body.

The first thing Ray saw was the hole in her head. Next was her hollow eyes—an image that would haunt him for many nights. She had chocolate skin. Her body showed signs of Rigor Mortis. There were droplets of dried blood at the corners of her mouth. She appeared to have been in her early twenties. Her figure revealed a beautiful young woman in her prime. She had her whole life ahead of her. Now, it had been snuffed out of her by men without conscience.

"Has any of her relatives or family contacted us?" Ray asked.

"None, no one has come to claim the body," Breya replied.

Ray stepped closer. "Doctor, can you tell us the time of death?"

"The autopsy revealed she died between 9 pm to midnight six days ago. She was last seen alive by an eyewitness at 9 pm that night."

"What else did your autopsy reveal?" Ray asked as he studied the corpse.

"I believe you've been briefed about it. We found cocaine in her system. But there is something else we discovered recently."

"What is it?"

"She has only one kidney."

"You mean one was removed?" Ray asked.

"It appears so, yes."

"But this was not in your initial report?" Breya said sharply. His face showed he was not happy.

"I'm sorry for the omission. Your team wanted to know the cause of death. The autopsy supplied that. We—"

Ray cut in. "Was her kidney removed recently?"

"The day she died? No."

Ray reached for the white sheet. He pulled it down and observed the body again. When he was done, he covered the face gently.

Breya glanced at him, hoping to hear what he would say.

"Breya, I'll like to take a look at the crime scene."

Breya heaved a frustrated sigh.

"I don't like this, but the boss said we should attend to all your requests." He stopped speaking and glanced at the medical examiner. "Thank you, John."

He turned to Frank and Ray. "Alright, guys, let's go."

***

Mararaba was a densely populated suburb on the outskirts of Abuja. Every morning, its busy road channels had traffic jams that stretched to eleven kilometres. The town was in the nearby state of Nasarawa. Still, its proximity to Abuja made it difficult to discern where Abuja's boundary ended and where Nasarawa's began.

The suburb was occupied by civil servants who worked in the capital city. These workers took advantage of low-cost houses and cheap apartments.

But the suburb was also notorious for a reason.

Over the years, it had become the melting pot for the dredges of society—cultists, armed robbers, hooligans, and prostitutes. Folk legend had it that your phone could be snatched from you in this neighbourhood even while you were holding it in your hand inside your car.

Ray and the rest of his team reached the crime scene at Mararaba Junction an hour and forty minutes later after being held by traffic. The crime scene was sealed with yellow tape and was surrounded by two policemen.

With his team, Ray approached the gutter where the victim was found. Out of habit, his gaze swept across his surroundings, and he quickly deduced why her killers picked this spot to dump her body.

An Okada rider carrying a plump woman braked hard to pass through a pothole on the road. Beside them were young men inside a sports betting shop wearing blue Chelsea jersey. Ahead, two kids hawking sachets of water passed beside a beer parlour. Beside them, an over-eager motorist disobeyed the traffic rule and parked his bus by the roadside.

A shrill voice drew Ray's attention back to where they stood. Someone was shouting 'thief', and the policeman they met at the crime scene ran to find out what was going on. He came back a few minutes later, panting hard.

"What happened?" Ray asked him.

"A young man snatched a woman's handbag. All her valuables were in the bag."

"Where is he?"

"He's gone."

"Call for back-up. Search for him," Ray insisted.

The policeman shook his head. "He's gone. This is Mararaba. Don't forget."

Such was the place, a neighbourhood filled with poverty and crime, where law and order had completely broken down.

Breya tapped his shoulder. "Ray, don't sweat over it."

Ray nodded and focused his attention on the crime scene.

"We found her body here," Breya said, bringing him back to the task at hand.

Ray moved closer to the empty gutter. "What time?"

"12 midnight."

"This place is always filled with people at any time of the day. It's possible that she was killed at another location, and they came here and dumped her body when fewer witnesses or no one was here," Ray said.

Frank nodded and said, "We assumed that she was killed here, but your observation makes sense. These are not terrorists who want to be recognised for their crime. They would prefer secrecy."

"Breya, you mentioned that the bodies you've picked up over the past three years had drugs in their system."

"Yes."

"And this is the first murder victim."

"Yes."

At that moment, a thought formed in Ray's mind. "This may not be the last corpse we will see in this case. Something else is going on here."

"Why do you say so?" Breya said.

"It's possible that they are trying to hide a crime or a bigger criminal activity. And now, they are tying up loose ends and killing the people who know too much."

***

At the same time, many kilometres away, at Ladi Kwali Conference Hall in Sheraton Hotel, the Abuja International Fashion week was taking place.

"Go, go, go!" Loretta said to her models backstage. The event started two hours ago. Now was her time to showcase her designs on the runway.

Within minutes, six young slim models began to catwalk through the flat, narrow platform with her first set of designs—women's ready-to-wear dresses. They looked tall in their high heels. The whole place was illuminated by blue lights and filled with an excited audience.

Each model stopped briefly in the middle of the platform to show the design to the audience. Camera lights from photographers beamed at them and captured those perfect moments.

From backstage, Loretta was watching the stage on a big screen with joy in her heart. While fashion was an art, it was also a business. She knew she was making a sales pitch by sending her models with clothes down the runway. A minute later, six models wearing her second set of designs—women's evening wear—came down the runway with poise and elegant confidence. Nothing was out of place.

Each of the models represented different ordinary women with their own poise and character. A single mother of three on her evening dress going to the grocery store. A young female secretary wearing a blue top and black blouse going to the cinema. A woman in love going to see her lover in the city. Loretta hoped the audience would see the same images in their minds.

When she was through with showcasing her own designs, a feeling of fulfilment swept through her. Within the next ten minutes, she became busy greeting her friends in the industry and some event organisers.

The Big Brother Nigeria superstar, Vivian, was there to shower her with praise. Vivian introduced her to celebrities and captains of industry. The experience was mind-blowing for her. A week later, critics would praise her designs for their comfortable yet elegant style.

By the time she got home in the evening, she was tired but realised that all her sacrifices were worth it. That feeling renewed her energy. She couldn't wait to celebrate with her staff. The Friday evening was time for her girls' get-together with Cynthia, and she couldn't wait to tell her all about it.

CHAPTER EIGHT

"Loretta, I'm sorry I missed the fashion show today." Cynthia's voice rang over the dining table at her apartment.

Loretta sipped from a bottle of champagne and said, "Don't mention. I know how busy you are at the hospital."

It had been a busy day for Loretta, but she couldn't miss the chat she always had with her best friend every Friday evening. This time, Cynthia was the host, and she was with her heartthrob and fiancé, Chuka Udoh, whom his friends called Chuks.

The round dining table was huge. The couple sat beside each other and snatched a kiss every few minutes, making Loretta feel like she needed to be with her own partner.

Ten minutes earlier, Cynthia had served them with white rice and catfish pepper soup. There were many things Loretta would have loved to tell her friend, but Chuk's presence hindered her. Yes, she'd known Chuks over the years, but this was strictly girls' talk.

Chuks was the kind of guy that only a girl like Cynthia could fall in love with. Six-feet tall, dark, and invariably well-dressed, Chuks was not particularly handsome. Still, he had a charm and excellent social skills that made him likeable. His mid-size unshaven beard was irritating to Loretta, but her friend treasured it. They appeared to be a love match—with their constant public display of affection.

"How was the show, Loretta?" Chuks' voice hovered across the room.

Loretta cut through a catfish with her knife and said, "It was an experience I would cherish for years to come.

I planned for it for weeks. It was definitely worth the effort my staff and I put into it."

Both Cynthia and Chuks gave her a reassuring smile. Cynthia glanced at her as she sipped from her own drink. "I know my friend. Babe, I'm sure you gave them a worthy performance."

Loretta blushed. Her mind replayed beautiful moments when members of the audience told her how much they loved her designs' creativity. She had already started getting purchase orders.

"Loretta!" Cynthia's voice boomed at her ears.

She snapped out of her reverie and looked at them. Confusion lined her face. They were standing, holding glasses of wine in their hands.

"Loretta, fill your own glass with wine," Cynthia said.

"What for?"

"We want to make a toast," Chuks said. His smile revealed his dimple.

"Okay." Loretta filled her glass with the bottle of champagne beside her and rose from her seat.

"First, let's make a toast to my best friend, Loretta," Cynthia said, "To success with her business. We wish her more victories and success stories. She will definitely become the most in-demand fashion designer in this city."

"Yes!" Chuks said. "Loretta, I wish you happiness and fulfilment in all you do. May you find the love of your life."

The last part took Loretta by surprise. She responded with a smile. "I'm making a toast to my friend and her fiancé. May this beautiful union end in praise and celebration."

The trio clicked their glasses and gulped them down.

They sat and slid into everyday conversation, chatting about everything and laughing whenever someone made a joke.

Loretta was enjoying the conversation until Cynthia held her hand, and silence returned.

"Loretta, Chuks and I are worried about you."

Loretta's brow furrowed. Where was this going? "You are both worried about me?"

"Yes, dear. I get it. You are single again. You made the right decision, and that's a good thing. But babe, you are working so hard and for what? You have no social life. I know you have some upcoming celebrities in your client list, but you are too buried in your work."

"We want you to go out, socialise and make new friends," Chuks said.

"Your life has reduced to a boring routine. In the morning, you go to work. You'd come back in the evening, and the pattern continues. Maybe you are following your ex-boyfriend Ray's life pattern—who is always quiet, never goes out, and has no friend that I know of. I never understood what you saw in him. I was glad when you told me both of you are no longer dating. Now, you need a breath of fresh air. Life is not all about work. Go out there and discover other exciting things about life. You are—"

Loretta cut in. "I don't have a space for all that in my life right now."

"Who said so? You are already growing popular if you don't know. You have started mingling with celebrities. You will benefit from this. You need to show up at the right places and make the right connections. It will benefit your career. I don't think anyone succeeds in the fashion industry by hiding at home. You need to be at the right parties, and I have just the right party for you."

"Uh-huh. Is this where all this is going?" Loretta was taken aback by her friend's words. "Which party?"

A smile flashed across Cynthia's face, and she slid a gold-coloured ticket across the table to her. "Now you are talking. It's an exclusive VIP party at the hottest place in Abuja right now. The event will hold tomorrow evening. Chuks got us invites. This place is frequented by celebrities and VIPs. You will be with the right crowd."

"It's going to be big. You will love it," Chuks said.

After five minutes of nudging, Loretta reluctantly agreed to attend the party. "Aaah, this may probably delay me from finishing my new project." She hoped she was not making a mistake.

As she greeted them and left, worry snaked up her spine as she thought of her friend. Yes, the couple seemed to love each other, but Chuks seemed to be all over the place. This was a guy who moved from one job to the next. Today he was working as a Personal Assistant to a politician. The next day, he was working as a Social Media Manager for a celebrity. He looked all good and perfect on social media.

Was that all about keeping up appearances? Cynthia had confided in her at one point that Chuks had no consistent income, but she loved him and provided for them both. Loretta didn't know the work he was doing these days, but it seemed to have given him many liberties. She hoped he wouldn't end up breaking her friend's heart. She got to her house thirty minutes later, and the moment her body touched her bed, she forgot about Cynthia, her charming prince, the planned event and slept off.

CHAPTER NINE

A phone call woke Ray from his sleep early in the morning. He quickly sat on his bed and shoved the grogginess away as he answered. "Ray Okon on the line. Who—"

"Ray, it's Breya. There is a new development in the case. How soon can you get to Herbert Macaulay Way?"

Ray became alert. "What happened?"

"I will give you details when you get here."

"Alright, I will be there in twenty minutes," he said and hung up.

He rushed to the bathroom and freshened up. Then he dressed and was in his car seven minutes later. The roads were empty, and he throttled up the vehicle speed to 120 kilometres per hour.

When he reached Herbert Macaulay Way, he called Breya and was directed to the crime scene. There, he discovered that a DSS agent was there already, along with three local policemen. He got out of his car and was startled when he saw the bodies. Five bodies. Two women and three men. All with bullet-holes on their head and their necks sliced open. They were killed gangster style.

"What happened here?" he asked Breya.

"I got a call this morning—5:00 am, to be exact. The agency phone operator rerouted the call to an awaiting call by a man, who identified himself as Nuru and claimed to have witnessed the crime. He said he called the agency as soon as he felt he was safe."

Ray's eyes brow furrowed. *A witness!*

"Where is this witness?"

Breya made a motion with his head for Ray to follow him. They walked straight down the road for five minutes, and then Breya stopped in front of a restaurant. The restaurant was still empty at that time of the day.

They entered, and Ray's eyes settled on a man who huddled himself beside a wall like he was feeling cold. Frank was with him. The man appeared to be in his early sixties. Tears were in his eyes. He heard their footsteps and made to scamper away, but Frank held him by his shoulder and spoke few words into his ears. When he saw clearly who they were, he relaxed.

"His name is Nuru Mustapha. I have not been able to ask him any question. He'd been sobbing, and we had to allow him to let it out and calm down. I believe he is much better now," Breya said to Ray.

Ray stepped closer to Nuru and knelt beside him. "Good morning, sir. I'm Ray Okon, a DSS agent. I believe you know who we are already. You can trust us. We are here to help."

Ray knew how hard it was for those in his line of work to establish trust with people who witnessed a crime. Some never talk. Others took time before they opened up.

The man's facial features softened, and he nodded in understanding as he wiped the last drop of tear in his eyes.

"Good. Tell us what happened there. You saw it happen, right?"

"Yes," Nuru nodded several times. "I thank Allah for my life. I could have been killed just like them. I am a mechanic. I have always been an early riser. My house is not far from here." He pointed his hand across the road. "Every morning, I do come out here to jog along the empty road. I love the calmness of this city, especially in the morning. It was when I was jogging that I saw them.

The way the vehicles braked hard and stopped quickly made me panic. I quickly went for a cover and watched it all from there. It was painful to watch."

"What happened? Who are they?" Ray asked. His prodding voice was gentle but firm.

"They came in two land cruisers. Six men with guns. They had black balaclavas pulled over their heads. I couldn't see their faces. The five people they killed were at the corner of this road at that time. I didn't know what they were doing there. They seemed to be on the run. From whom? I don't know. The men took them by surprise and shot them to death—all of them. Next, two of the gunmen, each wielding a knife, slashed the necks of their victims. As soon as they finished, they entered their cars and zoomed off. The whole thing didn't last for more than four minutes.

Ray raised his brow. "Jesus Christ!"

"How do we know the killers are members of the cartel?" he asked.

Frank said, "Nuru doesn't know about that, but he said he recognised two of the murder victims."

"Do you know them, sir?" Ray asked.

But Nuru couldn't answer again. Tears were back in his eyes.

'He said that two of the murder victims—both young women named Chloe and Natasha—worked as call girls at Lozano Motel in Kuchigoro."

"How did he know this?"

"He said he had gone to the motel several times in the past."

Ray paced the restaurant. This had gotten worse.

Silence settled in the room.

Breya broke the quiet atmosphere. "I will call Dr John and tell him to run an autopsy on the victims."

"What about the local policemen at the crime scene?" Ray asked.

"Frank." Breya glanced at Frank. "You know what to tell them. We are not going to give them all the details about the case."

Frank replied with a nod and left to get things rolling with the policemen.

Breya made calls to the DSS to come and take the corpses to the morgue. Next, he called Dr John and updated him about the new killings and told him to carry out an autopsy on the victims.

Ray followed his team members back to their DSS office building an hour later.

Today would be a long day.

By the time he reached their office building, rays of the sun had started brightening across the horizon and over the rooftops, and the roads were filled with vehicles and pedestrians rushing to work. The city had woken up.

He went across the road and bought *pap* and *akara* from Madam Ejima—a woman who had become his friend because of his steady patronage.

She came out by the roadside to sell them every morning. Her *akara* was garnished with stew and fish. He ate the breakfast inside the new office assigned to him. Next, he began to pore over the files on the case.

CHAPTER TEN

Cubana Lounge, Abuja

Tuface's song, Amaka, buzzed from the speaker of Cynthia's Mercedes Benz as the vehicle cruised past Herbert Macaulay Way. Chuks moved his head at the driver's seat, singing along with Tuface. Cynthia and Loretta sat together at the backseat. Both went crazy as Chuks changed the tune and started playing 'Case' by Teni.

Loretta's heart throbbed with excitement as they cruised through the city and headed to the Cubana Lounge, the exclusive VIP party venue. She observed the city through the car window.

Abuja was a different city at night. Streets light illuminated its beautiful landscape, well-manicured gardens, and luxurious hotels. Loretta had lived in this city for years and loved its serene atmosphere.

Tonight, she saw another part of Abuja she didn't know. Why hadn't she thought of this before? The painful summary of her life was work and no fun. Tonight, all that would change. She would set herself free.

Chuks slowed the car when he entered Adetokunbo Ademola Crescent. An electric banner flashing the name 'Cubana Lounge' sat atop the next building in front of them. He parked the car at the parking slot, and the trio stepped out of the vehicle. They were met at the door by three muscle men. Chuks flashed their tickets. Loretta and Cynthia watched as the men exchanged a whispered conversation.

Within seconds, the bouncers stepped aside, and they entered the lounge. The first sight that greeted Loretta's vision was the dazzling neon lights in different red, blue, and yellow colours. "Wow, this is…"

Cynthia's face lit up. "It's beautiful, right? You have not seen anything yet."

As they moved forward, Chuks kept greeting VIP guys every few steps. He seemed to know everyone around there. One of the organisers directed them to the VIP section, and they headed there.

The lounge was well lit, spacious, and screamed new money. The sitting arrangement showed the owners took note of even the tiniest details. It was apparent they cared most about the comfort of their customers. Loretta's gaze narrowed as she observed the crowd. Rudeboy Psquare, one of her favourite musicians, was on the stage performing live. The crowd were jumping up and down as they sang to his melodious tune—Audio Money.

Loretta's face flushed. "Cynthia, is this really one of the Psquare brothers? Am I dreaming?"

"I told you," Chuks said to her.

"Yes, babe, the party has started. Just enjoy yourself, babe."

Loretta joined the crowd as the infectious frenzy in the room swept over her. She didn't know when she began to shake her waist to the tune of the music.

Rudeboy Psquare finished and left the stage, and the crowd shouted 'Kokomaster' as D'Banj came on stage. Kokomaster, D'Banj's nickname, boomed in the air as the musician began to thrill the crowd. Loretta couldn't believe it. It was as if the organisers at the lounge were fulfilling all her fantasies. When D'Banj removed his shirt and began to sing 'Top of the World', she and the crowd went crazy.

D'Banj's voice rang out as he dazzled the crowd with his electrifying performance. For the next thirty minutes, Loretta was lost in the atmosphere, propelled by the room's super-charged energy. Sweat was all over her face despite the air-conditioner in the room. She stopped, moved to a less crowded corner, and made to wipe her face when a hand touched her.

"Loretta, we have been looking for you. Where have you been?" She turned in the direction of the voice.

It was Cynthia and Chuks. They held glasses of wine in their hands.

Loretta's face softened. "Enjoying myself. Babe, thank you so much for this."

"You're welcome. We have good news." Cynthia's voice was charged with happiness.

Loretta moved closer. "Okay, I'm all ears."

She watched as Cynthia reached for her handbag. She brought out a golden card which sparkled under the neon lights.

Cynthia handed the card to her and showed her the pre-wedding pictures on her phone. "Babe, it's finally happening. We are officially inviting you to our wedding."

Curious, Loretta opened the card quickly. The inscription 'Forever together' was branded on it. Next, she scrolled through the pre-wedding pictures on Cynthia's phone. In one of the pictures, the couple held themselves in an embrace as they stared into each other's eyes. It was clear that they were in love. "Wow, congratulations to you both." Loretta raised her voice over the crowd. "I'm so happy for you guys."

"Thank you," both said in unison.

Cynthia's face brightened. "We have started making wedding plans, but let me not bore you with the details. This is your night. Have fun, babe."

Chuks came forward and touched her shoulder. "Enjoy yourself, Loretta."

She nodded with a smile and watched the couple as they walked away, arms wrapped around each other's waist.

Loretta stared at the card again, and sadness washed over her. At that moment, all she needed was a drink. She walked to the bar section, and the barman—a young man in his mid-twenties, met her gaze and said, "What can we get for you, ma'am?"

"Fayrouz."

The barman returned with a bottle of Fayrouz and a glass which he handed to her. She filled the glass with the drink and gulped it down, feeling its cold swirl down her throat. Yet the drink couldn't save her from the conflicting thoughts raging in her mind.

Now, the crowd and the music no longer mattered to her. She just wanted to be alone. She would finish this drink and go back home. She filled another glass and took a gentle sip, then set the glass down. She felt much better now.

"Please, may I join you," a rich, baritone voice said.

Annoyance broke across Loretta's face. This was precisely what she didn't need tonight—a man already buzzed from too much alcohol, eager to score cheap points with anything in a skirt in hopes of getting laid.

She turned to put him in his place, but her words instantly fizzled into a gasp. He was light-skinned, tall with broad shoulders, had a well-groomed beard and strong chin. He looked powerful and oozed sex appeal in a way that set her body on fire.

Holy shit, her face flushed.

He was super handsome, and his appearance exuded power and the confidence of a man who could afford anything he wanted. His wristwatch and gold cuff link must have cost a fortune. He was closer to her than she thought. His masculine scent overpowered her and made her legs go weak. Her walls shattered instantly.

"My name is Johnson Omata, and you are…"

His words made her take a thorough glance. She recognised the name and face she'd seen several times on the television. Her breath caught in her throat, and butterflies fluttered in her belly.

His quick raking glance should make her take offence, not feeling pleasure.

Oh, please, get a grip, she lectured to her inner adolescent. She didn't know when she broke his gaze and looked down the floor. But she met his gaze again, and her breath became erratic as she took him all in. His deep, piercing eyes bore into her, molten with longing, and hot blood rushed all over her body.

He had appeared on Forbes, Celebrity Magazines, and popular TV programmes. She remembered watching him open his fifth real estate shopping plaza in the city. Was she dreaming? Salivating in front of him would be embarrassing. Women must have been rolling all over him wherever he went. She wouldn't be one of the notches under his belt.

His powerful body, sleek in his white designer shirt, which she observed had two of its buttons undone, was way too close. He was hotter in person than in the photo. She hated herself for feeling like a high school girl who finally got a chance to speak to her crush.

"Hi beautiful, I'm still waiting for your reply. I hope I didn't offend you," he said, a smile stirring through the corners of his mouth.

"My name is Loretta Olawale," was all she managed to say.

"Beautiful name." His voice melted through her body. He rested his hand on the hard surface where she placed her drink. "It's nice meeting you, Loretta."

"Thank you," she said. She watched as he ordered his own drink—Hero beer.

He sipped his drink while maintaining his gaze on her. "Do you come here often?"

"No, this is my first time. I'm always busy with work and unending projects. My friend dragged me here," she said.

"Oh, I know your type. Miss Independent Woman. I admire that quality in women."

She arched her eyebrows. "You do?"

"Yes."

"You must have plenty of them."

He shook his head. "Nope, I'm single. I have no lady in my life."

"You want me to believe that?"

"You can believe whatever you want. I'm telling you the truth. I'm taking my time to find the right woman. Right now, I think I'm making progress."

The way he said it made her chuckle.

"I love the sound of your voice."

"You can do better. Choose a better pickup line."

His face warmed into a full smile. They slid into easy conversation, discussing everything from his business to his view of the capital city, to politics.

When she told him she was a fashion designer, his face lit up. For the next twenty minutes, they discussed fashion and new trends in the industry. Loretta had never felt so alive.

It was as if they had known each other for a long time. He seemed to have knowledge about everything. Within seconds of meeting him, her mood brightened, and as they talked, she discovered they shared many things in common.

When they finally exchanged numbers, it was the most natural thing for them to do. He received a call and left afterwards while promising to call her later.

Loretta sent Cynthia a message and ordered a taxi that took her home. As she lay on her bed, she couldn't stop thinking about Johnson.

CHAPTER ELEVEN

Ray came to work the following day and headed to his office. He dropped his bag and collapsed on his chair. The bag contained files about the team's investigation on the case for the past three years.

His office was tiny, with a desk and a plastic chair. An HP laptop sat on his desk. A heap of files was already forming on his desk. He would tell them that he'd need a file cabinet. Soon, his office would be filled with paperwork. He loved keeping things in order.

The sky outside grumbled and the once bright weather transformed into a cloudy sky. They had just entered the month of June. Ray rose, peeped through the half-open window, and observed that light rain had started falling. The city was dark as though this was evening. He closed the window, and as he walked back to his seat, he heard a knock on the door.

"Come on in," he said out loud.

Breya entered, a tired look on his face. Sadness clung at the corners of his eyes. Something had happened.

"Morning, Breya," Ray said.

"Thanks. Please, Ray, let's meet at the briefing room." His colleague's voice was tight.

Something had gone wrong.

"What is it about?"

"Briefing room, please. Right now," he said and walked out of the office.

Ray followed him through the door and walked straight to the briefing room. There, he met Frank and Dr John. It was just the four of them. Ray saw the expression on the medical examiner's face and knew it was bad news. Whatever it was.

"Breya, what is going on?" Frank asked, his voice anxious.

"The witness has been killed," Breya blurted out.

Ray's pulse raced. "Which witness?"

"Nuru Mustapha, the only witness we have in this case. He witnessed the murder that happened two days ago and told us about it. Now, he is dead."

"Jesus Christ!"

"How did this happen?" Frank asked.

"He was killed gangster style. There was a hole in his head. His neck was sliced open. One of his neighbours called us this morning and gave us the news. The neighbour said Nuru had instructed him to call DSS if anything happens to him."

"The body is now in the morgue," Dr John said. "He has no family. His neighbour said he was once married but have been divorced for years. No child in the marriage."

"How did they know? I thought we had this under control," Ray said as he paced the room.

Breya tapped his foot on the floor and said, "The mistake we made was that we didn't give him protection. We thought he was not in any danger. I don't know how they got to him."

"Is the boss aware of this?" Ray asked.

"Yes, and he is not happy. The headquarters is turning up the heat on him. They want results, and they won't like this kind of news."

"This means the cartel is now aware that we are closing in on them."

"Yes." Breya flashed his gaze at John, "Doc, have you finished doing the autopsy on those five murder victims?

"The results are not yet out. It will be ready within two days."

Breya nodded and glanced at them. "Boss wants to see us on Wednesday. Here."

"Because of this," Ray muttered.

"Yes."

At that moment, the room turned into silence which dragged for a long moment. Ray's mind became active as it swept through the information he knew so far about the case. "If I can recall, Nuru told us two of the murder victims worked as call girls in Lozana hotel at Kuchigoro."

"Yes, you are correct," Breya said.

"Let's follow that lead and go there this morning."

Breya considered it. "Alright. These criminals think they are steps ahead of us. Let's turn up the heat on them. Let's go in the evening. You won't see anyone there now."

"Alright, evening it is," Ray said. Frank nodded quietly.

Breya glanced at John. "John, get those results ready."

"I will," John replied.

***

Lozana Motel was in a single-storey brick building in Kuchigoro—a small community in the capital city. The facility stretched like a students' hostel. Ray, Breya and Frank at arrived the Motel dressed in their casual uniform. They wanted to keep this tight and quiet. They didn't want to attract any attention. Kuchigoro was notorious for its low-rise buildings and piles of garbage that had become a big problem for the community.

The moment they entered the compound, the sights of beautiful young women wearing pants and bra covered their vision. A light-skinned girl smiled at Ray, perhaps hoping he would smile back and meet her to discuss business.

As Breya went to the lobby to meet with the receptionist, Ray took time to study the environment. It was a beehive of call girls and cheap rooms for a quick romp, no doubt. The question was: what else was going on here?

Breya came back and said, "Let's go. The receptionist has agreed to lead us to the manager's office. She said his name is Paschal."

They followed the receptionist, a slim young girl with a huge backside. She entered a dimly lit hallway. As they walked fast, they heard sounds of lovers in different levels of sexual activity. The groans and moans got louder when they reached a bend. She cut to the right and knocked on a door Ray guessed was the manager's office. The door opened, and they entered.

The man who opened the door was visibly angry. He appeared to have been in a bad mood and didn't like this kind of invasion.

"What is going on here, Martha?" he asked the receptionist.

"Sir, they are DSS agents. They are here to see you."

Breya stepped in. "Thank you, Martha. I will take it from here."

The young girl was already shivering with fear. She didn't say anything else but dashed out of the room.

"What the hell is—"

Breya flashed his credentials and cut in. "Sir, we are members of DSS Homicide and Anti-Drug Trafficking Unit. We are here to ask you some questions."

"About what? I am tired of paying endless taxes and bribing officers. This is extortion," Paschal fumed.

"Calm down. We are not here to cause you trouble. Just listen to us. We ask that you co-operate with us." Breya's voice had a calming effect.

Ray observed the man as the anger on his face faded. He went behind his desk and sat on the chair. "Alright, what can I do for you?"

"We are doing a criminal investigation. This particular incidence involves two of your workers—Chloe and Natasha." Breya dropped pictures of the two girls on the table. They had printed it out from the girls' Facebook page in the afternoon. "I believe you are aware that they are among the five people who were murdered along Herbert Macaulay Way two days ago."

Paschal's face tightened, the lines on his face visible. "Yes, my staff and I are still in shock over their brutal murder. Officers, who would have done this? This is wickedness." His voice was low and filled with emotions.

The man knows how to throw back questions to the face of his interrogators. Smart, Ray thought.

Breya nodded in agreement. "That's what we want to find out. Within the last few days, they worked here, did you observe anything strange in their behaviour or routine?"

"Chloe and Natasha stopped working here a month ago. The next thing I heard was that they have been murdered," he said and eyeballed them as though they were supposed to be aware of this.

"Really?" Breya arched his eyebrows and scribbled on his notepad. "What would have made them do this? Did you find out from their co-workers?"

"That was the first thing I did. They had no idea."

Silence settled in the office. Breya looked at his colleagues and gave them a look that meant this was a dead-end.

Frank stepped forward. "Mr Pascal, did they receive any strange visitors within the last three months they worked here?"

Paschal quipped in. "None that I was aware of it."

Breya dropped a card for the manager on the table. "Thank you for your cooperation. Please, contact us if you get any information that might help us in the investigation."

Pascal rose and collected the card. "I will."

As they headed to the door, Ray stopped and said, "Wait a minute," he told his colleagues. Breya gave him a puzzled look.

Ray went back and asked the manager, "Pascal, you must have a place where you kept a record of interviews and personal information about your workers. Can you recall where Chloe and Natasha worked before working here?"

Pascal considered this and said, "Let me check. A minute." He searched for a file on his desk. He found the white file and perused through it. "Oh yes, now I remember because then I thought it was strange, but I let go of the thought."

"What is there?" Ray asked.

"They both worked at hotel Monteziena in Italy," he said.

The agents raised their eyebrows. The puzzles, in this case, are rising like a storm, Ray thought, as they stepped out of the motel.

CHAPTER TWELVE

For the past two days, Loretta could not get Johnson out of her head. This morning, she woke up and found herself thinking about him, the way his lips curled up as he smiled, the confident look of his eyes, his deep baritone voice that set her body on fire.

Right now, I think I'm on the right path. I'm taking my time to find the right woman. His words echoed on her mind, and chords of desire raked all over her body. At that moment, guilt flushed all over her face, and she hit her fist on the bed and forced herself to stop. *What is so special about him? You don't know anything about him.*

She seemed to have calmed herself down, but she failed to calm the inquisitive spirit that suddenly became her constant companion. She soon became prey to the emotions coursing through her veins. The next moment, she didn't know when she began to check him out online. News about him was all over Google.

Famous businessman and philanthropist Johnson Omata visits the Super Eagles—and tells fans to stop criticizing and support the national team instead.

Africa's richest young entrepreneur, Johnson Omata, speaks with CNN Christina Amanpour on what it means to be an entrepreneur in Africa's complex business environment.

Real Estate Mogul Johnson Omata begins giveaway on Twitter, giving 100 young Nigerians ₦100,000 each, to start their own businesses.

Millionaire Entrepreneur, Johnson Omata, speaks on how he started his business empire with ₦5000.

With each new one, she saw herself delving deeper into his world. Gosh, she felt she was invading his private space. These were all the links she could click on to read the full article. She saw his Wikipedia page but scrolled past it. She scrolled down and saw a link that mentioned Johnson Omata's Instagram page. She clicked it open and scanned through it. She finally saw what she was looking for—his Instagram handle. Within the next minute, she was on Instagram checking his profile page. Her eyes were wide open as she scrolled through his pictures.

His designer clothes appeared to be custom made—just for him. They looked perfect on his body, she thought. She stopped to view a picture of him without a shirt. In the photo, he had just come out of a swimming pool. He was bare-chested. His body was all muscles—abs and six-packs. His arms dripping with water. Then her eyes settled on his long delicate fingers. At that moment, she could feel her core become wet as she imagined those long fingers on every part of her body.

She took a sharp intake of breath as her eyes closed on their own. He was the total package. *Oh, my God.* It had been long she felt the touch of a man. What would those sexy lips do on her body? The phone jangled beside her, interrupting her naughty thoughts. She picked it but didn't recognize the Caller ID.

"Loretta Olawale on the line," she said.

"I couldn't sleep that night we met."

Holy shit. Johnson.

She heard his voice and hot blood rushed all over her body. Her breath became erratic, and she forced herself to behave. Had she become a weakling? She hoped she was a superhuman with the power to get rid of all these emotions.

"Is this why you called me? To cry like a baby?" She was proud she was able to finally control her emotions. But then, he did what she didn't expect; he broke into laughter. Was he mocking her? "What's so funny?"

"I wish I can see your face right now." His deep voice made her blood whoosh.

She wasn't going to sit here and waste her time while listening to his ramblings. "Johnson, this is morning, remember. I'm already late for work. You have one more minute."

"Let me make it count. Be my partner at today's dinner party in Nicon Luxury Hotel. 8 pm. My driver, Peter, will come to your house and pick you up by seven-thirty."

"No!" she snapped.

"Why?"

"I'm busy."

"Whatever you are doing can wait."

"No, it can't. I won't disappoint my clients because of a request from an arrogant stranger." She found herself enjoying the argument.

"Now, I know why I admire headstrong women." His words caught her off guard.

She clenched her fists. "Is that what you call me? One of your women? You know what, get the hell out. I'm going to—"

"My lady, I'm sorry if I offended you. I overstepped my boundary."

There was something about his voice that always got to her.

"This is the only request I'll ever make of you. Please."

Silence. The moment dragged.

"Let me not waste both our time. I'm running late for a meeting as well. 7:30 pm it is," he said and hung up.

No! She wanted to say, but she didn't know why she felt a surge of delight all over her body.

***

The tension in the DSS briefing room was over the limit.

Their Station Chief, Ezekiel Bassey, had an angry expression on his face.

"I didn't expect this from you," he said and paced the room.

Ray sat beside Breya, Frank and the rest of the team members. They were all dressed in their complete DSS uniform. Ezekiel had just finished reading a report Breya gave him about their progress since they last met.

"The body count is piling up. And yet, we have not made any progress. I want results, not endless explanations."

Dr John entered the room and dropped a file on the table. "The autopsy report, sir."

"Summarize," Ezekiel ordered.

"It's the usual. We screened their blood for drugs. It's the same with the others; tramadol, cocaine and ecstasy."

"Anything else?"

"Ray asked me to check if their kidneys are still intact."

"And?"

"They are."

Ray had thought so as well. If the first murder victim had one kidney, it meant she sold it by herself months ago to get the cash. That seemed to be the latest craze these days.

"This cartel is becoming more violent every day. The headlines about these murders have started becoming a constant feature in our national newspapers. I want my men to close the gap on these criminals and bring them to justice."

"Sir, if I may..." Ray started.

Ezekiel cut in, "No!"

He glanced at the team leader. "Breya, get me results. Liaise with the police and other agencies if you must. I want a daily update."

"Yes, sir," Breya said.

"Good, this meeting is over," he said and stormed out of the room.

The rest of the team began to disperse.

Ray felt the tension. It was clear that their boss didn't want anyone's input in today's meeting. He was just here to give orders. This meant the headquarters were piling pressure on him, and he was transferring the same pressure on them.

That had become the norm in law enforcement agencies these days. And if these orders were not obeyed, heads would roll. But this case was not the usual case they dealt with. With Pascal's admission and everything their team had uncovered so far in the case, it was clear to Ray that this was more than meets the eye.

As Ray left the room and headed to his office, his phone rang, and he brought it close to his ear.

"Ray." It was Breya. His voice was on edge.

"Please, come to my office."

Alarm travelled down his spine. "What happened?"

"You need to see this."

CHAPTER THIRTEEN

Ray and Frank arrived at Breya's office at the same time. His office was modest with a mahogany desk, chairs, and a file cabinet.

"Breya, what is going on?" Frank asked.

Breya gave them his smartphone and said, "This message was sent by Paschal, the Lozana hotel manager. He promised to call us if he found any new information that would help us. He came through. I received this message a few minutes ago."

They read the text message. "I spoke to a friend of Chloe and Natasha named Miguel Odera. Weird guy. Never figured him out. He wants to talk. Meet him by 7:30 pm at 30 Binta road, Gwagwalada. Wear a casual dress. The man in the middle should wear red. Be with your DSS badge."

Frank gave Breya back his smartphone.

Breya glanced at them. "Get ready."

They nodded in understanding.

***

By seven-thirty in the evening, they were already at a dirt road beside 30 Binta road in Gwagwalada neighbourhood. Ray was dressed in a black jacket on khaki-coloured trousers, and Frank, who stood in the middle, wore a red polo on red trousers. Breya wore black jeans and a brown T-shirt with a yellow face cap.

Gwagwalada was a busy neighbourhood with stretches of row-rise buildings and an unending expanse of land. This was one of the first few neighbourhoods that greeted a visitor as he entered the capital city.

As development and building projects boomed in the capital city, this neighbourhood benefitted from the spill over. There were still empty lands and buildings under construction every few kilometres. But as far as Ray knew, real estate developers were on a buying spree in this place, purchasing every empty land they could see.

Ray and his colleagues waited for thirty minutes before seeing a small figure appear from afar and loomed larger as it approached them. The man was in his early thirties. His skin was the colour of charcoal. He reached where they were and fixed his gaze on Frank.

"Your badge," he said to no one in particular.

They all flashed their IDs. He examined them closely. "Follow me."

They did. Breya glanced at the rest, his eyes flashing at the Berettas holstered to their thighs.

Ray understood his message—the mission was dangerous, and they could be walking into a trap. Their team leader wanted them to be alert.

The man with no name cut right into a dirt road surrounded by thatched houses and huts. Very few knew this part of Abuja existed. The people living here were the Gwari tribe—the original owners of Abuja.

As Ray thought about this, his brow furrowed, and sweat formed on his temple. Why would this Miguel Odera be living in a place like this? Why would he want to meet them here? It was becoming obvious to him that this man might be in hiding. Who was he running from?

They strode past untarred roads filled with shallow water and dirt. Some of the residents saw them and came out of their tiny houses. This seemed like a place where everyone knew each other. They sure stood out like a sore thumb.

The man they followed zigzagged through different roads for the next ten minutes and then entered a big unpainted low-rise building. At the end of the long, cemented corridor was a door. A tall, thin man appeared through the door. He saw them and exchanged a few words with his friend, who nodded and entered the room.

As he approached, odour oozed from his body—a mix of cigarette smoke and something else Ray couldn't fathom. As he swept his eyes over him, it was clear that drugs had messed him up. His eyes were big and shallow, and he seemed to be hanging on the last thread of life.

"Follow me." His voice had lost its colour. They followed him as he stepped out of the house. As he walked, he looked over his shoulders, his eyes watching for an unseen enemy. His steps were unsteady, but he stumbled on and led them to a lonely road beside a Guava tree on the edge of a maize farm.

"You DSS?" he asked in Pidgin English.

"Yes," Breya flashed his badge. "And friends of Chloe and Natasha. Thank you for your courage. We appreciate the fact that you want to help us catch their killers. We—"

Odera didn't wait for Breya to finish. "I want protection and full immunity."

"We can work out a deal once you give us the information we are looking for." Breya's voice was calm and offered Odera the assurance he needed.

He nodded. "I can tell you everything you need to know about Dragon Cartel," his voice rang out.

Ray's eyes widened. Shock registered on their faces.

"Dragon Cartel?" Breya said.

"Yes, I was once one of their foot soldiers—a member of their death squad. Then, something happened, and I walked away. But no one walks away from the Cartel and gets to live. Now, they are killing everyone out there who knows their secrets."

So, this is what is happening, Ray thought.

"Tell us everything you know," Breya urged.

"I can give you the name of their leader," Odera said, and his eyes swept right and left, his voice on edge.

Would he reveal the identity of the cartel's leader?

Ray's eyes widened, his mind grasping the implication of this information they were about to receive. If they could get this information, they would solve this case once and for all.

Breya's gaze held Odera's eyes firmly now. Any misstep, this man would lock up and refuse to talk. Ray guessed Breya knew that and wanted to make sure it didn't happen.

"Tell us his name," Breya said.

"His name is..." A bullet flashed past the Guava tree and blew out his head, splattering pieces of blood and brain matter around them.

"We are under attack!" Breya shouted. The shooting started, and Frank grunted and fell.

"Ray, carry him and head inside the farm. Fast," Breya said.

Ray nodded. Odera was already dead by the time the rest of his body dropped on the ground. Ray dragged Frank inside the farm as Breya ran out to the road and started firing his gun where the gunshots were coming from.

Frank's clothes were drenched with his blood. Ray's heart raced, and he put his finger on Frank's neck and felt his weakening pulse. "Frank, stay with me."

At that moment, he heard a departing vehicle.

Breya ran back inside, panting hard. "They are gone."

His eyes zeroed on Frank, and he quickly brought out his phone and dialled a number.

Ray held Frank, "Frank is losing blood. We need to find transport that will take us to the nearest hospital."

CHAPTER FOURTEEN

Nicon Luxury Hotel, Abuja

At the same time, several kilometres away, Peter Mansour, Johnson's driver, was waiting for Loretta like a sentinel beside a black Lincoln Navigator.

He parked in front of her apartment and opened the passenger door for her. His black three-piece suit was so tight on his bulky frame. He lifted his bald head, his dark face expressionless as she approached.

Loretta wore a blue Ankara gown, three-inch stilettos and a ruby stone necklace. Her long braided hair framed her dimpled face. She had to stroll so she would not fall.

"Good evening, ma'am," Peter greeted as she held the door. She flashed him a warm smile and entered through the passenger door. He entered through the driver's door and drove the car down the road. When they reached the hotel, he parked the car across the road, opposite the hotel. Then he came down and opened the door for her.

"Where is he?" she asked.

"He is here waiting for you. Let me lead the way," Peter said, his voice gentle and polite.

She stepped down, and her eyes met the imposing building that housed the Nicon Luxury Hotel. The hotel sat three storeys high, right at the Capital city centre and adjacent to the International Conference Centre.

As she crossed the road, a new sight appeared in her vision, and she gasped as awareness travelled down her spine.

Johnson. He wore a blue round-necked long-sleeve Senator fitted shirt and matching trousers. His shirt had three straight top buttons. A ring-like string originated from the last one and connected to a golden button on his breast pocket.

He was super-hot, and his custom-made dress appeared to be fresh out of the designer's office. He approached her and took his time to appraise her with his eyes. His gaze bore into her, and she felt he was undressing her. "You look breath-taking." His voice was magical.

"Thank you."

He entwined her arm with his and led her into the hotel entrance, filled with people in colourful dresses. At that moment, a man in a tuxedo shook hands with him.

"Honey, let me introduce you to my great friend, David Attah. He is a stockbroker working with the Nigerian Stock Exchange." He paused and smiled at his friend, "David, this is Loretta." David appeared to be in his early thirties. He was dark and had a permanent smile plastered on his face.

"Hi, Loretta, it's so nice to see you. You look fabulous," David said as he greeted her and then shook hands with his friend. She thanked him, and they moved forward. Johnson introduced her to the Director of TVC News, a Senator and three real estate moguls. He seemed to be at home with everyone.

Camera lights flashed as they entered the big hall. Giant chandeliers hung on the ceiling, and conference styled chairs sat on the floor. The hall was filled with bigwigs and industry leaders. She saw representatives from the United Nations, Amnesty International and European Union. This was a star-studded event, and Johnson seemed to be in his natural habitat here. He would have been attending this event every weekend.

The event started ten minutes later. She soon discovered this was not a dinner party, as Johnson told her but an award ceremony.

"Ladies and Gentlemen, we want to recognize wonderful personalities who have contributed to our humanitarian effort and assisted us in our fight to reduce the suffering of displaced people in IDP camps," one of the speakers was saying.

Loretta raised her eyebrow, trying to understand what was going on.

"The Boko Haram terrorist attacks in Northern Nigeria has displaced thousands of people from their homes and deepened the poverty in the area. Over the years, we in Green Light Foundation have worked with the United Nations, many organisations, and the international community to provide relief efforts to people in these IDP camps. Today, we want to honour and recognize some donors who have assisted us with their huge donations and philanthropic efforts. One of such beautiful heroes is Johnson Omata. Please, sir, come to the stage."

Loretta's eyes raised as Johnson rose and advanced to the stage. A top UN director and the Green Light Foundation founder shook hands with him and handed him the award—a golden plaque with his name inscribed on it. The trio took group photographs, and Johnson's smile shone brightly as the crowd began to clap.

Loretta joined the rest of the crowd in the ovation as curiosity flashed through her facial features. By the time she set her gaze on the stage, Johnson was on the podium with a microphone.

"I'm honoured beyond words," Johnson's voice vibrated across the hall. "Thank you very much, Stella. You and your wonderful team at Green Light Foundation are the real heroes of the people in these IDP camps.

"Green Light is doing a noble work of reducing the inhumane suffering people in these IDP camps are facing, and we need more people and organizations to join and support their efforts," he said and paused for a moment. The crowd hung on his every word.

"I grew up amid slums and the worst poverty that no child should ever be allowed to endure. I was raised by a single mum who threw herself through hardship and depression to give me a chance at a better life. Over the years, as I made my own wealth through sheer hard work, my life philosophy can be summed in three words: pay it forward. When I see poverty around me, I have made it one of my primary life goals to help in the best way I can. The suffering in these camps is terrible. I knew the only way I could sleep well at night was if I helped put a smile on their faces.

"When I met Stella at the IDP camp in Maiduguri, and she told me about the work she and Green Light were doing. I knew they were the people I need to work with. Thank you, Green Light Foundation. I'm grateful." His speech was followed by loud applause.

When he stepped out of the podium, more camera lights flashed across his face. Loretta was speechless. She was seeing another side of him, and for her, this represented the best of the human spirit. He is so kind, she told herself as she wiped the tear in her eyes. His speech melted her heart.

After his speech, many other donors were called and given awards. When the award ceremony ended, classical music blared from giant speakers mounted on top of the wall. Loretta looked around her and observed that everyone was with their partner, dancing to the rhythm of the music.

"Do you want to dance?" His voice invaded her thoughts. She didn't know when she began to feel nervous.

"You were...at the podium..." her voice trailed.

He interjected. "May I?" She let him, and he took her hand and led her to the centre of the hall. When he placed his hands on her waist, sparks flew all over her body. They held each other close and flowed with the rhythm of the music. Johnson's huge body almost engulfed hers, and Loretta felt light in his arms. The solid weight of his arms on her waist made her aware of how fast her heart raced. She watched his Adam's apple as he swallowed.

When she averted his gaze, she discovered that almost all the couples were watching them with content smiles. Loretta wanted to stay on the dance floor forever as they swayed gently to the music. He sent her a look that had her heart dipping dangerously low. All too soon, the music ended, but he kept a light hold on her waist.

"You didn't tell me," she said.

"About what?"

They were so close to each other now, their body almost joined to the hip. She could feel his hot breath on her neck. "Forget it."

Her curious eyes met his, searching for answers.

"I love your speech," she started.

He fixed his gaze on her face. "I love your sexy lips." His words made her feel wet.

Suddenly, the hall felt stuffy and tight.

"Do you want to leave this place?" he asked.

"You know my mind," she said.

He flashed her his winning smile and led her out of the building. They crossed the road and saw Peter opening the passenger seat for them.

"Drive," he said to Peter.

"Yes, sir."

They entered inside and soon held each other's hands. Johnson stared at her and his fingers caressed through her hair. The simple touch ignited a fiery response in her body. The whole place was charged with electricity.

They could no longer deny the attraction that had been building within them.

Loretta's pulse raced, her eyes focused on his full sumptuous lips. At that moment, Johnson stared at her, his eyes shimmering with heat. He leaned closer and captured her lips with his mouth, and strands of heat charged within her, pooling at the wet place between her legs. She opened her lips and let him in, and their kiss became fierce. The kiss felt so good. It tasted sweet. Then he brought his mouth to her neck and trailed light kisses down to her nape, and a sharp moan escaped her lips.

He broke the kiss leaving them both panting hard. "Peter, take us to the house," he said and looked at her. She nodded. Her body was now a mass of needs and wants. He had flipped on the switch on her inner desires.

"Yes, sir," Peter replied.

She pulled his head closer to hers and brought her lips down on his mouth.

CHAPTER FIFTEEN

Gwarinpa Estate Abuja

Loretta and Johnson were in a rush as they fumbled with each other's buttons. They kept kissing until the vehicle stopped in front of the enormous building in Gwarinpa Estate. Gwarinpa Estate housed the single most extensive estate in Nigeria. It was a neighbourhood for the rich that sat west of the city centre. The area was urban and well developed, with tree-lined streets and large gated houses.

A gateman rolled the huge gate, and the vehicle entered inside the marbled compound. The car stopped in front of the house, and the trio stepped out of the Lincoln Navigator. Peter rushed and unlocked the glass door with the press of a remote button for his master and headed to his own living quarters, a two-room apartment close to the gate. Johnson led Loretta across the tiled hallway as they made their way to the bedroom.

Loretta's eyes shimmered with desire. This man had unlocked a spark within her. She couldn't wait to feel his body on hers. They sprinted past the winding staircase, and he led her upstairs to the door of his master bedroom. He opened the door and fixed his hungry eyes on her. Next, he captured her lips with his mouth, and she opened her mouth and allowed his tongue to delve deeper inside.

Her body was now a hot mess, and she wanted to feel his naked body on hers. He seemed to read her mind and pulled her closer to his chest. He groped her dress gently and helped her remove it. She tugged on his shirt, quickly unbuttoned it and dragged it out of the way.

Her fingers rapidly caressed his firm body, and her eyes squeezed shut as the sensation shot all over her nerves. She opened her eyes and observed that he fixed his hungry gaze on the big breasts caged inside her tight bra.

"Oh God," he let out a low guttural moan and unsnapped her bra, making her breasts bounce free. He suppressed a groan and latched his lips on the hardened nipple of her right breast. Loretta's head bobbed back, and fresh waves of sensation tightened her nipples and made her core drip with her wetness.

As though he was not satisfied, he broke free and fixed his lips on her left nipple, sucking it hard. Her legs became unsteady, and he carried her and laid her on his king-size bed. The moment they landed on the bed, he climbed on top of her, trailing light kisses from her neck to her chin. Goosebumps rose wherever he touched, and her clit throbbed in anticipation. She responded by gripping his belt. She loosened it and quickly removed his trousers and boxers. When her fingers latched onto his hard dick, her head went into overdrive.

"God, it's huge and hard as a rock," she said without shame as her fingers caressed it from root to tip. His dick became harder in her fingers, and she heard him grunt. He lost his patience and lowered his mouth, capturing hers in a fierce, demanding kiss.

She began to caress his hair, enjoying the best night of her life. Without warning, he spread soft wet kisses from her neck to her stomach, igniting the cells in her body. He held her smooth, slender legs .and she gasped when she felt his lips on her toes. He sucked each of her toes like a baby who had missed his mother's breast milk and parted her thighs to gain access to her pleasure palace.

When his hungry gaze met her underwear, he grunted as a burning desire filled his eyes. "Wow, a thong."

"You like it?" she blushed.

"You are full of beautiful surprises, my lady." He hooked his fingers on its rope.

She closed her eyes, treasuring the moment. Her body was flooded with heat. She desperately wanted release.

When she opened her eyes, she felt his lips on the side of her thigh. His wet kisses sent sparks all over her. Whenever she wanted his lips to dive straight to her groin, he would delay her pleasure and continue to spread light kisses across her thighs, driving her crazy. With each kiss, his mouth inched closer to her wet valley.

"No!" He had tortured her enough. She couldn't wait any longer. She slid her thong to one side with her fingers and shoved his head down her well of desire. When his lips touched the stiff nub of her clit, she arched her head back and gasped as tears of pleasure flooded her eyes. It had been so long since any man evoked such deep feelings in her.

Johnson's tongue lapped fast on her clit, and fresh wetness flooded her pussy. He didn't stop. He parted her slick, wet folds with his fingers and inserted two digits inside her. She responded by bucking into him to bring his fingers deeper inside. His expert fingers moved faster inside her, and she rode on them as her body built to hot pleasure. Needing the touch of his lips, she pulled his head up and captured his lips with hers as she clung her naked body to his.

The sensation she felt seared every cell in her body. She couldn't wait for him to sink his hard dick into her wet depths. "Come in, please, right now."

He fixed his gaze on her. "You are sure?"

She responded by latching her fingers on his cock, caressing the precum that had appeared at its tip. He spread her legs wide and brought his lips down her wet valley, his tongue lapping fast on her wetness. She spread her thigh wider as she surrendered totally for him.

He drove his tongue inside her swollen folds and sucked hard. She held his head with her hands and guided him, making sure his tongue touched all her pleasure spots. Then he broke free, panting hard, and his right hand gripped the foil packet of a condom on his bed stand. She watched him, hoping he did it fast. He snapped open one of the foils and rolled the condom down his hard rod.

She spread her legs to accommodate him. The moment he drove inside her slick folds, stars split in her eyes.

"You are so tight," he grunted in a husky voice as he drove every inch of his dick inside her.

She held his bareback tight with both hands, her breath coming out in short bursts. He amped the rhythm of each thrust, fucking her deeper all the way to the hilt.

She let out primitive sounds calling his name as he marked her body with his hard thrusts. Within minutes, they maintained a steady rhythm.

She felt it coming. She was getting closer. "Harder," she screamed.

Johnson increased his thrusts' intensity, pounding in and out of her as her huge breasts bounced without restraint. Then, he flipped her over and guided her as she climbed on top of him. She glided her big hips down the length of his long dick and rode him hard. At the same time, he held her tight and feasted his lips on her right nipple.

"Johnsooon!" Pleasure exploded in her groin, sending her into a hot, fulfilling climax. He tightened his grip on her body as he released spurts of liquid joy into the protective foil that covered his rod. She came undone in long-lasting spasm and collapsed on him, both well spent. She climbed down from his body and lay close to him. He cuddled her in his strong arms, and she felt comfortable in his warm embrace.

CHAPTER SIXTEEN

Victory Hill Hospital, Gwagwalada

Ray battled with dark memories of yesterday's events as he sat in the waiting room inside Victory Hill hospital in Gwagwalada. Beside him were tired-looking Breya and their boss, Ezekiel, who came in thirty minutes ago.

They had rushed Frank to the hospital here immediately after the shooting. Both he and Breya slept in the waiting room last night. Now, it was seven in the morning and rays of sunlight had started filtering through the cracks of the window. The room was filled with metal chairs and anxious relatives waiting to hear the news about their loved ones' fates.

A TV screen that hung on the wall was playing a romantic Nollywood movie.

Ray figured it was a hospital tactic to give the anxious loved ones the escape they needed. In his own case, it failed to lessen his anxiety over Frank's health condition. He shifted his eyes from the TV and stared at the white paint at the wall as horrible memories from the night before invaded his mind, landing at his heart with a heavy thud.

"Frank, stay with me," he had pleaded. They had located the Victory Hill hospital through the directions given to them by the neighbourhood residents. It was close to eight in the evening. In the hospital hallway, Frank lay on a stretcher surrounded by nurses in blue and white tunics. Ray and Breya walked closely behind them.

"We need to get him to the emergency ward now," someone was saying.

Both Ray and Breya followed the nurses and a doctor whose name tag read, 'Victor Fedayo'.

"No, sir, you can't enter here." Ray was held back by one of the nurses as he attempted to enter the emergency room.

"What is going on?" Breya queried the moment he joined Ray at the door. Ray quickly explained the situation to him.

"We are DSS agents. The patient is our partner." Breya fumed.

"I don't care if you are VIPs. Do you want us to treat your partner or not? Allow the health experts to do their job. Go to the waiting room and stay there. If your attention is needed, we will call you," the angry nurse said and pointed to the left. "Once you reach that end, take a right, and enter the next room you will see. The loved ones of other patients are there. Obey the hospital policy. Everything will be fine."

Breya wanted to protest, but Ray held his hand and led him to the waiting room. It was a crazy evening. Ray knew the stress had gotten to his partner. Anyone who had the same experience would be on frayed nerves. But first, they would need to allow experts to do their job.

Within ten minutes of staying in the waiting room with eyes filled with worry, Dr Victor entered and pointed at them to follow him. They rose at once and increased their pace to close the gap on the doctor.

"Doctor, what is going on?" Breya's voice was tinged with anxiety.

Ray glanced at Dr Victor, whose expression was calm. He had an air of competence around him. He must have gone through this stage with hundreds of patients—holding news that might either bring relief or shatter lives.

"He is lucky. The bullet fractured his libs," the doctor said in a practised, measured voice.

"So, Doctor—" Breya made to quip in.

The doctor cut in. "If it had moved five inches closer, the bullet would have hit the spinal cord. If that had happened, he would never walk again."

Ray heard Breya mouth "Thank God" under his breath.

"Doctor, what do we do now?" Ray asked.

Dr Victor brought out a document. "He is unconscious. We need to take him to the theatre right now. We need to do surgery and remove the bullet. Who is his next of kin?"

"He has no known relatives. We are his partners and closest friends. I can sign, sir," Breya said.

"Alright, sign here," the doctor said and gave him the document and used the ballpoint pen to show him where he would sign. Breya scribbled fast and gave him back the form.

"That will be all for now," Dr Victor said and left.

Breya made to ask him another question, but Ray held his hand and signalled him with his eyes to let it go. Breya grunted and staggered to his seat. Ray stood there for a long moment before he made his way to the chair. Throughout the night, he forced himself to sleep, but the same image was on his mind.

I can tell you everything you need to know about Dragon Cartel. The next thing he saw was a bullet ripping off Odera's head. He was their sole witness.

The words echoed in his mind. Someone shook him, and he opened his eyes. The sun shot its furious rays at him, blurring his vision. He wiped his eyes, and his vision began to clear. Once they were clear, he observed Breya staring at him. He met his gaze, and Breya nodded knowingly and signalled him to follow his eye. He did and saw their boss sitting beside them. At that moment, awareness travelled down his spine as he discovered that this was morning and they were still in the waiting room.

He glanced at his boss and observed the blank expression on his face. He didn't need a seer to tell him that Ezekiel was furious at them for screwing up yesterday's operation. They messed up big, no doubt.

"Any word from the doctor since he went for the surgery last night?" Ezekiel asked.

"None," Breya said.

Silence settled among them as they waited. Ray took that opportunity to sweep his eyes across his surroundings. More people poured inside and settled on the empty seats.

"No, I want to see my wife," a man who stood outside the door groaned in a bitter voice.

"Not yet, sir, her corpse will soon be released to your family."

"No, I want to see her now. I want to see her one last time."

"Sir, your sister is with the twins in the recovery room. Please go and see your new-born kids."

"No! I can't believe Monica is gone."

Ray heard the painful moans. He fixed his gaze at the heartbroken father and saw him break down in tears. Hospitals. He didn't want anything that would remind him of his own past. A drop of tear appeared in his eyes, and he looked away. At that moment, a man in a white coat entered through the door and started walking in their direction.

"That's the doctor, sir," Breya said to Ezekiel, his voice anxious.

They rose as Dr Victor reached where they were. He shook hands with Ezekiel and greeted them. But Ezekiel quickly dispensed with pleasantries. "Doctor, our agency is already aware that one of our agents is in this hospital. My bosses have been calling me, but I can't give them any new information concerning his condition because I don't have any. Please, how is he now?"

"We removed the bullet last night. He is out of surgery. Sorry for the delay in getting back to you," the doctor said.

Ezekiel and Breya heaved a sigh of relief.

Thank God, Ray said silently to himself.

Breya stepped forward. "Please, sir, when can we see him?"

"Unfortunately, you can't see him today. We have stabilized him, but he is still unconscious and needs medical attention. Give it a few days. Once he wakes up, you will be the first to know."

Ezekiel greeted him in a firm handshake. "Thank you, doc."

The doctor left after that, and the three men strode out of the hospital. As Ray and Breya escorted their boss to his vehicle, he stopped and said, "Go back to your office. I will send men who will stay with Frank here in the hospital. Once he wakes up, they will let us know. The men will also act as his security. We are not leaving anything to chance."

"Yes, sir," both men replied.

"Breya, get me a report about yesterday's operation this afternoon."

"Yes, sir," Breya said. They had only given him a summary of what happened.

"What's the name of that cartel again?" Ezekiel asked.

"Dragon Cartel," Ray said.

Ezekiel nodded, entered his vehicle and drove away.

Ray joined Breya in another car, heading back to the agency. The name he just mentioned left a bitter taste in his mouth and reminded him of the unfinished business in this case and the damage this cartel had done.

His jaw tightened with his firm resolve. They now knew the name of the criminal cartel and had put a name to a faceless enemy. For Frank and all the victims, Ray would join his team and hunt these criminals down wherever they might be, and he wouldn't stop until they were caught and put behind bars.

CHAPTER SEVENTEEN

At the same time, inside the Penthouse building in Gwarinpa, Loretta awakened after a satisfying sleep. Memories of their lovemaking the night before flooded her mind, and her lips curled in a smile. Her right hand moved on their own accord and reached for him.

Confusion surged through her when her hand touched no bare muscled body. She lifted her face and glanced at her side. He was not there. Where was he? She dragged herself from the bed and wore her bra. She picked a big towel on the bed, wrapped it around her naked body and sauntered out of the room.

As she ambled through the hallway, her eyes rose in wonder as she observed a reflection of herself on the transparent walls covered in stucco paint. Expensive paintings showing beautiful views of River Niger hung every few meters on the wall. She took a right and ambled through an open French door that led to the living room.

The décor in the living room looked like something out of a presidential suite. Glass covered the surface from floor to ceiling. A massive 4K resolution television screen—the kind she had seen only in cinemas, was fixed at the centre of the wall. Celine Dion's 'My Heart Will Go On' blared from the walls, but she didn't see where the speakers were mounted.

She strolled past the transparent tiles and stepped out of the door, entering a small balcony. She peeped through its slightly open window, which revealed a panoramic view of the city.

Far ahead, she saw the golden dome of the National Mosque and the Millennium Towers, which glittered under the June morning sun. At that moment, awareness surged through her, and she discovered that she stood semi-naked while almost outside the house. She stepped back inside but didn't know where Johnson was. The whole place was confusing to her.

"Johnson! Honey," she called out.

"I'm right here," his voice rang out.

She followed the sound of his voice and soon strolled into the room she deduced was his kitchen. Surprise registered on her face as she stood at the door and watched Johnson peeling yam. He is full of surprises, she thought, and she loved every part of him he'd shown her.

She stayed there and drank him in. Her mouth hung open as she watched the fluid movement of his strong arms. The beautiful sight stimulated memories of their intense lovemaking, which was still fresh in her mind. She closed her mind as she remembered how he held her gently in his strong arms. She had slept peacefully in his arms afterwards. It was a night she would always cherish.

As she watched him peel the yam, a gradual realization bore into her; she had fallen helplessly in love with him. This was precisely the spark she'd been missing in her last relationship. Now, she didn't want any other man. She wanted Johnson. Her body came alive under his gentle touch, and he made her feel like a woman.

He turned and stared at her, and she resisted the temptation to meet his gaze.

"Good morning, beautiful," he said and began to slice the yams and put the tiny pieces inside the pot.

"You are here," her voice was soft and unsteady.

"Yes, I told my housekeeper not to come today. I want to prepare a special breakfast for my lady."

My Lady. Her body trembled as she heard his words. Suddenly, it was as though her tongue was tied. She didn't know what to say. She stayed there and watched him until he finished boiling the yam and preparing stew which he garnished with egg.

"Honey, breakfast is ready. Let's go to the room." His voice melted her core. It always got to her in a way nothing else could. They sauntered to the room, and he set the two plates of food on the bed and placed a spoonful to her lips. Her mouth parted for him, and he fed her. He held her gaze and watched her as she ate the food and swallowed. There was something about his eyes and the way he looked at her—it was intense. Loretta felt it could pierce through her soul.

As he stared at her and bit his lips, hot blood rushed through her pleasure spots and her body hungered for his touch. At that moment, the sound of a ringing cell phone broke through the spark building around them. He pulled the bedcover aside and brought a Samsung smartphone to his ear.

"Yes, talk to me." He listened for a long moment and said, "Yes, do it," and continued to listen.

Loretta thought she noticed steel in his voice—there one minute, gone the next. Was she hallucinating? She didn't hear his last words before he dropped the phone on the bed stand.

"Honey, what is it about?"

"It's nothing, darling." His voice carried an assurance that brought her relief. He pushed the two plates of food aside and pulled her closer to his chest. Her soft lips opened to protest, but he covered it with his lips. Sparks flew across her brain, igniting every cell in her body. *Oh my God*. She didn't know when she let out a sharp moan.

"Baby, what are you doing? We need to eat," she said between hot kisses. Her heart was racing.

"Exactly, baby, you know what I need right now."

"What? It's not that—"

He stopped her mid-sentence with another kiss.

She resisted, but his hands roamed her body and settled on her breasts. Her resistance wobbled.

"Baby, I want us to eat first," he said in a hoarse voice.

"Alright, but let's eat food first. I—"

Her words turned to moan when he unsnapped her bra and latched his hungry lips on her hardened nipple. Within seconds, he entered inside her, and they had another love-making that blew her mind away. Afterwards, they continued their breakfast. As Loretta was deep in thoughts of her new blossoming love life, his voice brought her back from her reverie.

"Baby, I'm having lunch with my mother on Wednesday. Please, I'd like you to come with me." His voice registered in her mind, and her heart throbbed.

He held her chin with both hands and said, looking into her eyes, "Baby, please, join me. This is a big step for me. For us. I know this is going too fast. I can't stop it."

Suddenly, a frown appeared on Loretta's face.

"Baby, what is it? Talk to me."

"If this is your formula, then count me out of it. Your mum must have met all the women in your life by now," she hurled the words at him.

"No." He moved his hand defensively. "I have never introduced any woman to my mother before. She wants to see the woman in my life. This time, I just want it to be a surprise for her."

Loretta's pulse raced. This was a big step, yes. Relief flooded through her. This meant he felt the same way she did about him. "Yes, but just this once..."

He didn't wait for her to finish. He kissed her hard, and she rested her head on his chest the moment they parted their lips.

CHAPTER EIGHTEEN

DSS Office, Abuja Central Branch

"What more do we know about Dragon Cartel?" the voice belonged to Ezekiel Bassey. The question was more for the benefit of the new visitors in the room. The briefing room was charged with tension this morning, partly because the Yellow House—the unofficial name for the DSS headquarters, sent two of their top analysts to the meeting.

Ray sat beside Breya and the rest of the team, dressed in his complete DSS uniform. One of the analysts was a man in glasses called Clement Owolabi. He was a legend in the agency who developed a database DSS used in tracking criminals. His partner was Anderson Okafor, a tall, muscled man in his mid-forties. They came with a modem they connected to one of the laptop computers in the room.

Tight lines appeared on Ezekiel's face. He was under immense pressure. Rumours were already flying about that he might be axed soon enough. When Ray heard it, he hoped it was not true. This was not his fault.

"What we know about them is still the basics. They deal in illicit drugs, including Tramadol. They pump these drugs into the city's bars, motels, night clubs and hotels. They also control prostitution rings in Italy and Dubai, where they lure innocent Nigerian women seeking greener pastures outside the country. We have no evidence yet to nail them on this neither do we know who they are. Recently, we made progress when we finally discovered their name. We've put Odera's name in the agency's database to know if we will get a hit. Before he was shot dead, Odera confessed he worked with the cartel. He could have given us a major lead on these criminals, but they got to him before he talked to us," Breya explained.

Clement stared at the screen and said, "The guy that was shot, what's his full name?"

"Miguel Odera," Breya replied.

Clement nodded and worked on his laptop, his fingers punching the keyboard furiously. After three minutes, a smile appeared on his face. Ezekiel and Anderson shot him a curious glance.

"Come and see this," he said to them.

They came closer and stared at the laptop screen.

"We got a hit," Ezekiel announced, looking up. "Please, Clem, bring it up to the screen at the wall," he said, and everyone in the room looked up as two images appeared on the bigger screen.

It was a picture of two men who appeared to be in their late thirties or forties captured outside a night club. Both held a bottle of wine in their tattooed hands. They were in a celebratory mood. Ray quickly recognized the thin man in the first picture—Miguel Odera.

"This new database is using an updated software recognition system. The man in the first picture is your man—Miguel Odera," Clement lectured. "The second man goes by the alias Raze Brown. We don't know if that's his real name. Both are long-time friends. The interesting part is that Raze is the manager of Glorious Heights Night Club. He is a street dealer who has been distributing drugs in the city through his secret networks. For years, we've been investigating him but never found any evidence that linked him to his criminal activities or the cartel he was working with. Now, we know the truth."

Ezekiel stared at the two pictures. The tight lines of his face had faded. "Odera confessed he has worked for the Dragon Cartel and disclosed he wanted to bring them down. If he has been friends with Raze Brown, who was known to supply these drugs, then we can presume they both worked for the Cartel."

"You are right. They are definitely birds of a feather," Anderson said as he glanced at him.

"Right now, Raze may have the information we are looking for," Clement said.

"But the question is, what is really going on in the cartel right now? Why are they killing their own people? If they are trying to tie up loose ends, why now?" Breya asked.

Clement glanced at Breya. "That's what you and your Unit should figure out as soon as possible."

"Yes, sir," Breya replied.

"Ladies and Gentlemen," Ezekiel's voice had regained back its confidence. "Raze is our next lead right now," he turned to the two analysts. "Thank you, Clem and Andy." He shook hands with them. He turned to Breya, "You and Ray will go to Glorious Height this evening. Find Raze wherever he is."

"Yes," both Breya and Ray replied.

As the two analysts began to depart, a phone rang, and Ray watched as Ezekiel picked the call. He listened for a while and turned to face them. "Frank is awake. We will see him at the hospital tomorrow morning. Right now, our priority is Raze Brown. Find him," he ordered.

Ezekiel faced everyone in the room. "Start hitting your keyboards and your contacts. I want to know everything you can find out about Dragon Cartel."

***

By Seven in the evening, Ray and Breya were in his Camry racing to Glorious Heights Night Club, located in the central business district. They were shocked to discover this nightclub operating right under their noses. Yet, no one knew about the illegal activities going on.

Abuja Central District stretched from Aso Rock in the east to the National Stadium and Old Gate in the West. It was the city's power centre, dividing it into the northern sector with Maitama and Wuse and the Southern sector with Garki and Asokoro. Tall buildings and skyscrapers housing the headquarters of Multinational Corporations sat gallantly on both sides of the highway.

They drove past the Three Arms Zone and soon entered Shehu Shagari Way, which sat across the Tomb of the Unknown Soldier. They took a left and entered a narrow road that led to the club. Ray observed the quiet street, which appeared to be a residential area. There were few houses here and few humans on the road.

"We are sure it's this street?" he asked Breya.

Breya stared at his car's GPS. "Yes, 13th Roland Noel Street."

The car slowed down as the road curved like a snake and straightened as they got closer to the club. Breya parked the car by the side of the road and killed the engine. They alighted from the vehicle and approached the building.

The building was colourful in red and white paint as Ray stared at it from afar. But when they came closer, they discovered that it was deserted. No single soul was lurking anywhere around the building. No club activity was going on. It was as though Glorious Heights never existed.

"There is no signboard to indicate that the club was once in this building," Ray observed.

"Check this out," Breya beckoned to Ray. He was at the entrance of the building.

Ray stepped onto the little terrace. The place was not dusty. "There was human presence here recently."

Breya nodded, observing the same. He turned the doorknob, but it was locked. He inserted a bobby pin inside the small hole on the doorknob until it reached the internal locking mechanism. Then, he turned it and unlocked the door. The door creaked open with a hard shove from his shoulder.

"What the hell?" Breya said. They stared in stunned silence. It was the club alright. But everything had been scrapped recently.

"They acted fast and closed down the club. That should be a few days ago," Ray said.

"Then, where is Raze Brown?" Ray asked.

Breya closed the door, his face lined with exhaustion. Ray stepped down from the terrace, and a new thought hit him. They parked out recently and wiped everything clean. Who warned them? He didn't know why he didn't spot this earlier. The patterns were apparent. They had a leak in the agency, perhaps, in his own Unit.

CHAPTER NINETEEN

That same evening, Loretta lay on her couch, resting after a busy day at the office. She was finally back to her house after spending a wonderful time with Johnson at his plush apartment. The beautiful memories they created together flashed through her mind, and warmness enveloped her body. They had been in constant communication since then.

Today, while at the office, she found it hard to concentrate. It was Jane who saved her day and made sure she didn't miss a crucial meeting. Now, she was discovering how difficult it was for her to banish him completely from her mind. At that moment, her phone pinged a blue light, and she clicked the new message open.

"I miss having you in my arms, baby. – J.O," the message read.

She read it and chuckled. She texted back. "Naughty boy, allow me to concentrate. I'm busy working on a new design."

She lied. She missed him crazy.

"You should rest. You have a busy day. Don't overwork yourself, my lady. J.O," came his reply.

She attempted to text him back, but her doorbell chimed, and she rose from the couch and ambled to the door. She opened it and was faced with a furious Cynthia.

Cynthia held a celebrity magazine in her hand. She wore a long weave and looked stunning in her Ankara gown and blue handbag. Even though she was angry, her friend was a beauty queen anytime.

As Loretta made to welcome her, surprised registered in her face when Cynthia pushed her aside and walked straight to the couch. Loretta joined her and sat beside her.

"Welcome, babe, please sit."

Cynthia remained standing. Instead of sitting down, she threw the celebrity magazine on her laps. "Girlfriend, this has been going on, but you never told me."

"What is…" Loretta's words hung in her throat as her eyes fixed on the magazine, and she saw a picture of her and Johnson standing arm in arm at the dinner party at Nicon Luxury hotel.

"I…we…" she stuttered and stopped making a wasted effort as her face flushed.

Cynthia eyeballed her. "Good, you didn't deny it," she said and sat down.

Loretta muttered something incoherent.

"He's hot. You look great together."

Loretta's eyes flashed with delight. She finally found the will to speak. "Thank you, babe."

Cynthia quickly stared at her. "Is that all you have to tell me?"

Loretta intertwined both her hands. "I'm sorry, I didn't tell you earlier," she paused. "I don't know how to begin. Everything is happening fast. We met that day at Cubana lounge."

Cynthia sat upright. "Oh, you met each other at the lounge? I remember when Chuks noted that you left abruptly that night without informing us. I later saw your text, where you said you were heading home and wondered why you didn't call. After then, I called you to make sure you got home safely, but the call didn't go through."

"I was with him that night. We met and clicked right away. It was as if we've been together for years. I don't know how else to explain it."

Cynthia's face brightened. "Wow, I'm so happy for you, babe."

Loretta beamed. "Thank you. I know I can always count on you."

"Loretta and Johnson have started trending on Twitter. I guess his fans saw the picture of you and him together," Cynthia blurted out.

Loretta arched her eyebrow. "Really?"

"He is a popular guy, kind of a celebrity, remember. He has thousands of fans on Social Media."

Loretta didn't reply. She was still speechless as her mind tried to process the news she heard. Their love story had travelled far and wide.

"He invited me to meet his mother," Loretta heard herself saying.

Cynthia raised her eyebrow. "Babe, this is huge. He is really serious about you."

Loretta flashed her friend a wide smile.

"My gut tells me he is a responsible man," Cynthia said. "Babe, I got your back."

"Thank you," Loretta said and hugged her friend tightly.

"I'm so happy right now. My life is finally at the right place," Loretta said to her friend.

Cynthia nodded in understanding. "I know how it feels," she paused for a long moment. "Remember that my wedding is next week Saturday."

"Yes, I do, our-soon-to-be-bride. Which chief bridesmaid would forget something like that?" Loretta said, and her cheeks glowed into a warm smile.

"You know what, bring him to the wedding. Both of you should come."

Loretta's face curled into a full smile. "Thank you, babe. I appreciate this."

They slid into small talk, and Cynthia departed five minutes later.

Loretta settled back on her couch and soon got enveloped in her own thoughts. At that moment, tears brimmed at the corners of her eyes. Mum would have been so proud of me, she thought. She wished her mother was still alive right now. Now, she had the money to take care of her. But fate snatched her away from her so early. She'd missed her—her lovely smile—her encouraging words even when she battled with severe problems in her own marriage.

You have fire in your eyes. The words surfaced from her memories, merging her past and present into one...

"Mum, how do you do this?" a twelve-year old Loretta asked. Her pretty, young face raised to where her mother sat while sewing clothes with her sewing machine. In her mother's shop, she observed every move her hands made. She weaved tiny fabrics together and transformed them into fashionable garments that her customers loved.

Her mum understood her question and smiled. "My daughter, I use fabric, wool and this machine," she stared at her daughter and beckoned. "Come closer, honey."

The young Loretta came closer and sat on a bench beside her mother's sewing machine.

"I practised for years until it became a part of me. Don't worry, you will be a great woman. You have fire in your eyes."

Loretta nodded and smiled at her mum. As her mother patted her back, the young girl's gaze settled on the fresh bruise on her mother's neck.

Her cell phone beeped, bringing her back to the present. She read the message. "A reminder. We have lunch with my mother tomorrow. I can't wait to see you again. J.O."

She read it. Newer memories pushed away the pain from the past burning at the back of her mind and gave her the gentle peace she needed right now.

CHAPTER TWENTY

Victory Hill Hospital, Gwagwalada

The next morning, Ray, Breya and Ezekiel arrived at the hospital. They were in haste and walked fast into the building, escorted by a nurse in a blue coat who already knew who they were.

Ezekiel had a meeting with some politicians in an hour. So, they wanted to do fast and leave as quickly as possible. The three men first went to Dr Victor's office. Ray and Breya waited outside the door of his office as he and their boss spoke in the office for fifteen minutes. When he came out, Ray glanced at him and observed that he was in high spirits.

"Let's go," Ezekiel said. They followed him, and the same nurse led them to Frank's ward, where he was recovering and getting treatment.

Frank was eating food from a food flask when they entered. He saw them, and his face glowed with excitement. He was on the bed. The drip attached to his arm had recently been removed. The heart monitor was no longer in the room. A bandage covered a large chunk of his stomach.

"How are you doing, Frank?" Ezekiel asked as soon as they settled down on three plastic chairs beside his bed.

"I'm doing fine, sir. I'm so glad you guys came," he flashed his eyes at Breya and Ray. "Thank you both for saving my life."

Breya raised his head to protest, but Frank still had words in his mouth. "Dr Victor said you both acted fast and rushed me to hospital on time. It made a huge difference. I'm grateful to the agency for taking care of my welfare."

"I hate myself for allowing this to happen," Breya said.

"No, you are the best team leader, Breya. Thank you."

Ray leaned closer. "We are glad that you are recovering fast. We can't wait to have you back on the team."

Frank face brightened into a wide grin.

Ray held his hand. "Our promise to you is this: we are going to find the criminals that did this. We are going to make sure they pay for their crimes."

Breya left some banana and pineapple on top of a stool close to the bed. Ezekiel dropped a fat envelope from the agency.

They departed five minutes later and reached their Abuja Central branch in twenty minutes. Ezekiel's secretary had told him on the phone that politicians were waiting for him in the office, and he rushed to meet them. Breya shook hands with Ray and went to see the analysts working with their team on the case.

Ray told Breya he would soon join them. The expression on his face was blank when Breya looked for an explanation on why he didn't want to join them. He repeated what he said, and Breya left afterwards. Ray advanced to his destination. He had an important task to carry out.

***

Ray waited for his boss in his secretary's office. Martin had told him he was in a meeting with two members of the House of Representatives. He asked Ray if he should come back another day, but Ray had declined politely. This was a sensitive issue. He relaxed on the seat Martin offered him and tried to organize his thoughts. This was the first time he would be seeing his boss twice in a month. This is necessary, he reassured himself.

Two hours later, the door opened. Two pot-bellied politicians in white flowing *Agbada* dress poured out of the office, escorted by his boss. They chatted and laughed as they walked through the door.

Ezekiel came back four minutes later and flashed him a curious glance. "Agent Ray, my secretary told me you've been waiting for me for the past two hours. This must be a serious matter. Please, come inside."

Ray followed him inside the office. This time again, he insisted they should stay on the sofa.

"Coffee," Ezekiel offered and pressed a button on his desk.

Ray attempted to refuse, but Martin soon entered the office and handed the men cups of coffee.

As they took their first sip, Ezekiel said, "Ray, what is it?"

Just like his boss to get straight to the point, which worked fine by Ray.

"Sir, I discovered that since this investigation started, the Dragon Cartel has always been one step ahead of us."

His boss' expression hardened. He clenched his jaw. "This is common knowledge in the agency. The failure of your Unit has brought me huge embarrassment. Is this what you came here to tell me?"

"They know our every move," Ray continued.

Ezekiel interjected. "Then fix it. Catch these criminals, for god's sake."

"I won't be surprised if this has been going on for a long time," Ray said.

Ezekiel made to cut in but held his tongue. He sensed his agent had more to say.

"Sir, we have a leak."

Ezekiel's mouth dropped open. "What?"

"We have a leak in my Unit. We have a rogue agent who is working with this cartel, giving them sensitive information on every move we are making on this case."

Ezekiel's face was set in a worried look as he listened.

"Sir, a troubling pattern has emerged in this case. We will get a witness, and before he can talk, he will be killed. How does the cartel know this? Who gives them this information? All our witnesses have been killed," Ray said.

Ezekiel remained in stunned silence. His expression showed Ray he knew what he said was true.

"I studied the case files and discovered that this has been going on for the past three years."

Ezekiel leaned closer, his gaze showing the new clarity in his eyes. "Odera was killed a few days ago. In the report your team gave me, you said he wanted to reveal the name of the leader of the Dragon Cartel before he was shot dead."

"Yes, sir."

"Who else knew about the text message Pascal sent to your team informing us that Odera wants to talk?"

"Apart from you and my team members, no one else knows about it, sir."

"This means that no one else could have known that your team would meet Odera at Gwagwalada by that time."

"Yes. This implies that one of the people who got this information passed it down to a member of the cartel."

Ezekiel nodded, his face tightened as the implication of this settled in. When he looked up after a long moment, he said, "We've been compromised."

"Yes, sir," Ray said.

"But there is no evidence yet. How do you plan to find out who this rogue agent is?"

"I have an idea, sir."

"Go on."

Ezekiel listened as Ray spoke for the next five minutes.

Ezekiel smiled. "A brilliant plan. But it is complex and prone to errors. If that happens, the agent will become aware that we are onto him, and he will destroy all the evidence linking him to the cartel," he glanced at Ray. "I prefer the simple old school method."

He and Ray used the next ten minutes to fine-tune the plan until both were satisfied it would work.

Ezekiel looked at him and said, "Let's keep this under wraps. We will assemble a small team. You will have access to everything you need. You have my orders to go ahead with this operation."

"Thank you, sir," Ray said and stepped out of the office a minute later. They would need to do this right. The clock was ticking.

CHAPTER TWENTY-ONE

Nyoko Restaurant, Abuja

"My son, you have eyes for good things," Caroline Omata's voice hovered above a table at Nyoko, a big-shot restaurant at Tafawa Balewa Way.

Johnson, who sat opposite his mother, flashed her a wolfish grin. "Thank you, mama." He held Loretta's hand and whispered in her ear. "I told you she's a lovely woman. I know you will like her."

Loretta giggled and held his hand under the table. They were eating lunch at the restaurant. They had arrived thirty minutes earlier and waited for Johnson's mother, who came ten minutes later. She apologized for the delay. Caroline had taken a flight from Lagos to Abuja. The moment she entered and reached the table where they were, she hugged her son and kissed Loretta on both cheeks.

Caroline was a light-skinned woman in her mid-fifties. She had a towering, intimidating figure with deep, piercing eyes that reminded Loretta of her son. Her skin glowed, and it was clear that her son was taking care of her.

Johnson had told Loretta that his mother lived in Festac, in a duplex he'd built for her. His mother raised him by herself after his father impregnated her and left them, afraid to take on his responsibility. Johnson had grown up hating his father, blaming him for the suffering he and his mother passed through.

Despite the wealth she now enjoyed, Loretta could observe the deep lines on Caroline's face, traces of the poverty and hardship she endured while raising her son.

Loretta was glad Caroline was alive to witness her son's success, unlike her mother, who left too early. It showed on her face, especially when she looked at her son with tender eyes. She is proud of him, Loretta thought. Which mother wouldn't?

Soon after they all settled on their chairs, they were served with grilled pork, chicken sausage, and cervelat, garnished with mash, bruised cabbage and gravy sauce.

Now, their plates were empty, and they sipped lemon juice and engaged in light conversation.

"Loretta, you are the fashion designer my friends in Festac are talking about. It's nice knowing my son has a woman of substance in his life."

Loretta heard the words and glanced at Johnson's mother. Her words caught in her throat. She didn't know many people already knew her in Lagos. She was surprised that Caroline took such an interest in her. Her words were more of a statement than a mere comment meant to flatter her, a trait she shared with her son. "Thank you, mama. How did you know I'm a fashion designer?"

Did Johnson tell you? She glanced from Caroline to Johnson.

Johnson sensed her thoughts and raised his hands in self-defence. "I told her nothing, honey. My mother is a lover of fashion."

Caroline smiled. "I watched a replay of Abuja Fashion Week on TV. That's where I saw you. I love those designs your models wore."

Abuja Fashion Week. That explains it—what a small world. Loretta's face flourished like a rose flower revealing her perfect gap-teeth. "Thank you, mama."

Johnson's comment about his mother's interest in fashion made Loretta sweep her eyes over Caroline's dress. She wore a patterned green and white flowing 50's sleeves Ankara wrap dress which stopped at the ankles, interlaced with Rhinestone details and huge side pockets. A silver necklace adorned her neck and she wore black heels that supported her six-foot-feet frame. She was a fashionable woman, another trait she shared with her son.

Caroline's words broke through the silence. "Johnson, when are you coming to Lagos? Are you coming tomorrow for my friend's house-warming party?"

Johnson remained quiet as his mind worked to come up with an answer for his mother. Loretta looked subtly from mother to son. It was clear Caroline was not expecting a 'no' from her son. Her voice was authoritative.

"Mama." Johnson stretched the last letter as he held his mother's gaze.

Loretta relaxed on her seat, enjoying the mother-son drama.

"Oh, I know what you will say," Caroline said as her shoulder fell.

Johnson ran his hand over his head with a tired look. "Mama, I'll be busy this week."

Caroline regarded him with a stern face. "Don't do this to your mother, Johnson. You are the chairman of the event. Your presence is needed. I can't disappoint her." She looked away.

"Please, mama, you know how crazy my schedule is," he said. "Tell Mama Adebisi that I will call her. I will visit next week, I promise."

Her expression softened. "Make sure you do."

As Johnson nodded with a smile, Caroline stared at the couple. "I will soon be on my way to the airport to catch a flight back to Lagos to help Mama Adebisi prepare for her housewarming party." She flashed Loretta a wide grin and touched her hand across the table. "My daughter, it's so nice to finally meet you. I told my son that I must come around and see for myself.

Johnson had never wanted to commit to any woman. I was afraid this would go on for a long time. I'm glad that thanks to you, he changed his mind."

They greeted her, and the trio ambled out of the restaurant after Johnson paid the bill and dropped a big tip for the waitress. He called down a taxi for his mother. The cab would take her to Nnamdi Azikiwe International Airport. She entered the cab, and the car lurched forward into the busy road.

Johnson and Loretta saw each other every evening that week. On Saturday, both were at St Patrick's Anglican Church for Cynthia and Chuks' wedding. Johnson watched from one of the pews. As the chief bridesmaid, Loretta stood beside the couple at the altar as they exchanged their wedding vows.

***

On that Saturday afternoon, Ray and six DSS agents hand-selected by Ezekiel Bassey, who wore their black-on-black uniform along with a black bulletproof jacket bearing DSS in large white letters, arrived at Breya's apartment at Central District.

It wasn't hard for Ray to figure out the suspect in their Unit.

Apart from him and the boss, three other people were aware of the information to locate Miguel Odera at Binta road in Gwagwalada that day. Pascal, who'd sent the message, Frank, who'd been shot during the operation and Breya, their team leader.

He had dug into the case for the past three years and discovered that a deadly pattern had been playing out since this investigation began—witnesses turned up dead before they could talk. All of these happened under Breya's watch, and no one was smart enough to make the connection.

Now, they would find out what exactly was going on. Breya lived in a rented two-bedroom apartment, inside a three-storey building, in a quiet neighbourhood. The team located his apartment. One of the agents set off the alarm at the security panel beside the door. At the same time, Ray worked on his door with his lock pick set and pushed it inside forty seconds later. They entered and flipped the switch. Luckily for them, there was electricity. Their boss kept Breya busy, inviting him to attend a board meeting at the headquarters which would last until evening.

"Spread out. You know what to look for. Let's make this quick," Ray ordered. The men moved into the rooms with lethal efficiency. Ray knew Breya saw himself as an agent who had connections in the agency. He figured everyone knew he was clean. No one would ever suspect him of giving vital information to the enemy. If he was doing any illegal activity, his house would be the place for him to hide them.

The men worked for the next hour, looking under the bed, the red rug, carefully sifting through every part of the apartment, including the kitchen.

"Please, come and see this," one of the agents said.

CHAPTER TWENTY-TWO

Ray moved from the kitchen and joined them in the room he thought was the bedroom. But no, it was too tiny and bare. A storeroom? He stared at the small opening in the wall. "A safe."

"Yes," the agent who found it replied.

Fortunately for them, it was not state-of-the-art. They worked on the safe for five minutes and unlocked it. Ray observed that its cover was large. They had to break part of the wall to bring it all out.

The agent next to the safe put his hand inside and brought out two devices.

"What is it?" an agent behind Ray asked.

Ray's eyes flashed at the two objects. His jaw fell. "A burner phone and a flash drive."

"What is an agent doing with these two devices?" one of the team members asked.

"It's definitely an agent who has something to hide," Ray said.

The team went back to the living room. Ray went straight to the desktop computer that sat close to the wall. He gave one of the agents the flash drive. "Steve, boot the computer and slide in this flash drive. We need to find out what's in there."

The agent named Steve nodded and started working.

Ray switched on the burner phone and checked its call log. Three calls—all from the same number.

He dialled the phone number and put it on speaker.

"Dear customer, please, the number you are calling does not exist," a female voice chimed in his ear.

Ray shook his head and was about to drop the phone when his eyes caught a sent message in the text message box. "Call not safe. Can be tracked. Stick to our online backchannel," the electronic note read.

He showed his team members the text message. "How can we access this online backchannel? Does anyone have any idea?" Ray asked, his frustration mounted. This was getting more difficult than he thought. They had spent an hour and thirty minutes here and needed to leave.

"What about the flash drive?" an agent beside him said.

"Yes, the drive," Ray glanced at Steve. "Steve, what's in there?"

"It is protected with a password. Any message inside the drive is probably encrypted."

Ray stared at the desktop screen. Breya surely had everything set up. "I know who to call to get this information." He rose. "Alright, guys, put everything in place. Let's leave go. Good work, guys."

***

Breya stepped out of the DSS Headquarters outer building with Ezekiel Bassey and waved at junior agents. He was experiencing his best day in the agency, and he loved it. The day had been spent from a boardroom meeting to a debriefing section with senior DSS agents inside an air-conditioned conference room. At noon, he sat with his boss and officers from Abuja military police, Customs, Police and NDLEA. They enjoyed great jokes and were treated to a sumptuous lunch.

He was glad that Ezekiel had seen the light. His eyes had finally opened, and he had seen Breya as a resourceful agent who could even represent him in the headquarters.

Right now, Breya was enjoying every minute of this rare walk in paradise. He joined his boss in convoy with flashing lights and sirens that would take them back to their own branch in the central district.

The vehicle he sat in drove fast, and they arrived within twenty minutes. The passenger door opened, and he alighted from the car and stepped into cloudy weather that was threatening rain. It was four in the evening, and he wanted to get to his office and pack up for the day.

A group of five DSS agents led by Ray approached him as he walked boldly into the building. He grinned at them, thinking they were a welcoming committee.

"Ray, have you—"

"Breya Adams, please, remain calm. This is part of an ongoing investigation. For now, we have no option but to bring you in for questioning," Ray said and glanced at his men, and they held Breya and cuffed his hands behind his back.

"Wait, wait." Breya's jaw clenched. This can't be happening, he thought. "What is the meaning of this? You will all answer for this," But he became speechless when the station chief stepped out of his vehicle. Their eyes met, and he made his way inside the building. As Breya's blood boiled, fear crept into his eyes. Was today's events all part of a grand plan to get him arrested?

The men dragged him inside the building, and three minutes later, he was locked inside a detention room.

"I didn't commit any crime. What the hell is going on here? Nobody is telling me anything. Somebody should talk to me." His voice blared through the metal bars of his cell.

CHAPTER TWENTY-THREE

"This is a Threema Weblink," Tony Okafor said to Ray on the phone on Monday morning.

"What is Threema?" Ray asked, sitting at his office desk. Since Sunday, he'd been working with his friend, Tony, to decode the information on the flash drive.

Tony was once a famous whiz kid who developed an App for the Ministry of Health to detect fake drugs. He studied at MIT, United States, in a scholarship sponsored by the Nigerian government. When he graduated, the government fixed him in National Intelligence Agency. The country had lost so many bright kids like this—a brain drain that had been bad for Nigeria's economy. They didn't want to lose Tony as well. Today, Tony was a top analyst at NIA.

When Ray called Tony for the first time on Sunday and explained what was going on, they set up a meeting in the evening at a bar in Nyanya where they met over drinks. Ray gave him the flash drive. Tony hacked the device's password and saw the link inside a notepad embedded in a zip file.

"Threema is an encrypted messaging app that can be used anonymously by people to chat on its network. Users can use the Threema web to chat with other users on their desktop. That explains the link. Threema has end-to-end encryption that secures all communication within its network. The link should take us to the users' chat room. Threema uses the open-source NACI cryptography library for encryption. The encryption keys are generated and safely stored on users' devices to prevent backdoor access. I'll need three days to decrypt it."

Ray rose and paced his office. "We don't have three days. We are in the middle of a criminal investigation. If he is one of them, then I guess they would be communicating daily, perhaps at a particular time in a day. If they send a message and he didn't reply, they will deduce he has been compromised and will get farther ahead of us. Please, Tony, this is a priority."

"I will see what I can do," Tony said and hung up.

Three hours later. Tony called as Ray was in his boss' office. "Ray, this is huge. A lot has been going on here. I have decrypted the chats. Will forward it to your email"

"Thank you," Ray said and hung up.

He powered his PC, which sat on the desk in the office and opened his email. He saw an unread message. Tony is quick, he thought. This was why he loved working with him.

"What is..." Ezekiel said and stopped as they read through the messages.

Anonymous Sender: Nuru talked. He may be a problem for us.

Anonymous Receiver: Where is he now?

Anonymous Sender. In his apartment. I put a tracking device on the new phone I bought for him.

Their mouths hung open as they read the messages.

Anonymous Sender: Odera wants to talk.

Anonymous Receiver: He had been in hiding.

Anonymous Sender: I know where he is.

Anonymous Receiver: Where?

Anonymous Sender: For this information, my fees have doubled.

Anonymous Receiver: If it is accurate. Done.

Anonymous Sender: 30 Binta road, Gwagwalada. 7:30 pm. I will be there with my colleagues. Channel my funds through the same account.

"Jesus Christ, this guy has finished us," Ezekiel said.

Anonymous Sender: There is a complication.

Anonymous Receiver: What?

Anonymous Sender: One of my colleagues, Frank, was shot.

Anonymous Receiver: Collateral damage

Anonymous Sender: Tell your men to lay low for a while. DSS is all over it.

Anonymous Receiver: Can't promise you anything.

"He has betrayed us," Ezekiel said, his expression tight.

"Wait a minute," Ray clicked a button and moved up. Shock registered on their eyes as they read messages dating back to the past three years—all of them were information about the case.

"Print out everything!" Ezekiel fumed.

Ezekiel made a call, and Ray got busy with the evidence. Thirty minutes later, they walked to the detention room. They met Oliver Russet at the door. He was a DSS interrogation specialist who knew every pain nerve-ending in the human body.

"Oliver, thank you for coming at such short notice," Ezekiel said and greeted him in a firm handshake.

"Let's begin," Oliver said. He held his tools under his arm.

They entered the cell, and Oliver showed the handcuffed Breya the documents. Ezekiel had briefed him about the case before he came—giving him only the details he needed to know.

Breya looked worn-out. Dark circles had appeared around the corners of his eyes. Since Saturday, he had been locked in the cell. The guards were only allowed to push in his breakfast and dinner through the door. But no one had talked to him for over forty-eight hours—a standard interrogation technique meant to weaken the suspect's will.

Oliver read out the messages for Breya and dropped a document containing the decrypted messages on the table where he sat. "Breya, what can you tell us about this document?"

Breya gritted his teeth and struggled within his handcuff. "I know nothing about this. I am not working for any cartel. I have never committed a crime. This is a setup. I am innocent."

Breya stuck to his denial for the next hour.

Ray left his cell as Breya's cries filled the atmosphere. He strode to his office, closed the door, and sank on his chair. A deep-seated rage crawled up his spine, heating up his entire body. He took a deep breath to calm himself down.

His eyes settled on a framed photograph that he got from his study at home a week ago and hung on his wall. His uncle, Simon, a man who took care of him after his parents' death, had given it to him. Simon died of a heart attack five years ago.

The framed photograph was a picture of his parents. Both looked serene and so in love, never knowing the horrors lurking in their shadows which would destroy them in years to come.

Ray never knew his mother, Jessica. She died while giving birth to him. His father, Paul, died in a hit and run accident when he was ten. Or was it an accident? He then went to live with Uncle Simon. Simon took the case to the police. It made newspaper headlines then.

Ray would never forget the painful memories. But after two years of working on the case, the police ruled it as an accident. The driver who hit his father was never found. In a country with no security cameras, criminals often took advantage of the loopholes in the system to commit crimes in broad daylight.

As he grew up, Ray hated criminals. He wanted to fix the broken system that paralysed law enforcement agencies in the country. That was why he studied criminal law and joined DSS. Putting criminals behind bars would not make him forget the past but it would help ease his pain.

Part of the reason for his unnatural calm was that he had been putting a lid on the rage boiling inside him since he was ten.

Loretta had been the only one who broke through the wall he built around himself. Since she left, he had tried to bury his head in this case and forget about the heartbreak. He had tried to move on. But there were times when the feelings would creep in, and he would remember, and then he would miss her so much.

He broke into a sad laugh as he thought about his unique situation. The rogue agent who betrayed them had refused to talk. The case was going nowhere.

This was a case that made him forget her and move on.

But now the memories had rushed back—her Oscar-worthy smile, delicate face, the intense fire in her eyes and the feel of her skin.

He had proposed to her, and she rejected him. He had moved on. Had he? Why was he thinking about her now? My God, where is Loretta? He thought. What would she be doing right now?

CHAPTER TWENTY-FOUR

Several kilometres away, two sweaty figures moved fast in a perfect rhythm. Both were joined together at the hip. Tears of ecstasy appeared in Loretta's eyes as she held Johnson tight, scratching her nails across his back and gliding her hips up and down his hard rod.

"Right there, baby. Faster," Johnson groaned and fell back on the bed, giving Loretta the freedom she needed to blow his mind away. She placed her hand on his stomach and moved her hips down the length of his dick.

"Babyyyyy. I'm close!" The words escaped her lips. She rode him fast until they both exploded. Loretta closed her eyes as her groin became so wet. She climbed down from his body and fell hard on the bed, taking time to calm down the fast pace of her heart rate.

Johnson pulled her close and used his fingers to wipe off the sweat on her temple. To her utter surprise, he rose and carried her to the bathroom. She giggled and hung her arm across his shoulder, kissing him softly as the water from the shower cascaded across their soapy bodies.

"I love you," he whispered.

"I love you too, honey." She felt her body vibrate as she said the words. She had given herself completely to him, and she felt him open and became vulnerable in a way he had never been before. They showered in between soft kisses and came out of the bedroom ten minutes later. She dried her body and put on his oversized T-shirt and shorts, inhaling his scent as she sauntered to the kitchen. She prepared Amala and Egusi soup for lunch, and they fed each other in the dining room, enjoying the precious moments they had come to love.

"Sweetheart, please, be quick and join me in the bedroom," Johnson said in a husky voice as Loretta took their empty plates to the kitchen. Her face was filled with joy she wanted to hold on tightly to. She washed the dishes and ambled to the bedroom, wondering what surprise Johnson had come up with this time.

The moment she opened the door, she gasped and covered her mouth with her hands. Johnson knelt on one knee, holding a diamond ring in his hand.

He fixed his heavy gaze at her. "Sweetheart, the first time I saw you, my heart sent me a silent message, and I knew right then that you are the one for me. You have captured my heart with your warmness and inner beauty. I don't have to pretend when I am with you. You have set my heart on fire. Only you can quench that fire. Honey, I can't imagine living the rest of my life without you. Please, will you be my wife?"

Loretta was still in deep shock. Oh my God, her heart fluttered. Johnson had taken her unawares. But nothing was more powerful than the love she had for him. It was genuine and sincere, and all-consuming. She felt it in her heart. "Yes, yes!"

Johnson rushed over, carried her to the bed and crushed his lips on hers in a hungry, urgent kiss.

An hour later, Johnson uploaded a picture of Loretta's ring finger with the sparkling diamond ring on Facebook, Instagram, and Twitter. The image had the caption, 'And she said yes.' Three hours later, *Johnretta* started trending on Social Media.

***

"You sent this message to them. This is how you communicate with the Dragon Cartel, isn't it?" Oliver's voice hovered in the detention room.

Beside him was Breya, who spat out blood.

Ray was back in the detention room the next morning. Breya had refused to talk and stuck to his story. Sweat glistened across Oliver's face. His khaki shirt was folded at arm's length. Oliver had requested Ezekiel's permission to use more advanced interrogation techniques to get the suspect to talk. Still, he was told to hold on.

Breya's hands and legs were tied, the ropes digging into his skin. He had a broken tooth, and blood dripped from his lips. He appeared weak, but his eyes still bore the defiance Ray had come to observe about him.

"Breya, I hope you know this is treason. The punishment is a death sentence." Oliver allowed the words to hang in the air.

Ray watched from the bars of the cell. Breya remained silent. What was giving him confidence? He thought.

"If you tell us what we need to know, we will get you a reduced sentence," Oliver said and resumed. "Who are the people you are giving the information?"

"Who is the leader of Dragon Cartel?"

"You have over 10 million Naira in your three bank accounts. That is odd for a DSS agent. We have frozen the bank accounts. Is this why you betrayed your fellow agents and put one of your colleagues' life at risk? He almost died in the hospital."

Ray watched Breya's expression. The words hit him hard. His body jerked violently.

"I want my lawyer," he barked.

At that moment, a hand tapped Ray on the shoulder. "Agent Ray." Ray turned back, and his eyes met Martin's. "Chief wants to see you."

Ray followed him and climbed through the stairs. They reached the second floor, and he soon got his boss' office. The door was wide open. He had been a constant visitor here lately. He entered and met Ezekiel reading a document with glasses.

Ezekiel saw Ray and stopped.

"Welcome, Ray, please take a seat." He motioned with his hands for Ray to sit opposite his desk.

Ray knew his boss had been busy since Breya's arrest and had been in constant communication with the yellow house. Many in the agency were still shocked that a rogue agent had been among them all the while.

"Ray, you are now the leader of HATU. This is official and has been approved by the agency."

The news blasted at him like a bullet. He knew his boss loved cutting to the chase. But this came out of nowhere. Ray was speechless.

"The information you uncovered from Breya's communication with the Dragon cartel is shocking. All these while I worked with him, I never knew he had sold us to the enemy. The agency is aware of the progress you have made in this case. They want you to take charge and hunt these criminals down. Well done, Agent, on an excellent job."

"Thank you, sir."

Ezekiel glanced at him. "Frank has been given a one month leave to enable him to recover. But he insists he would stay away for three weeks. Due to experience, I wouldn't want to assign many agents to your team. You will work with the analysts here in our branch. They will give you all the support you need. If you need extra help, I will assign you a small tactical team to help you get the job done just like you did when you invaded Breya's house. Frank will join you when he gets back."

"Thank you, sir."

"That will be all, Agent."

Ray rose and walked out of the office, feeling the weight of his new responsibility on his shoulders. There was much work to be done. He wanted to pull the rug right under the legs of those criminals.

CHAPTER TWENTY-FIVE

The door of the studio of Starlight television network opened halfway, and a chubby woman from the control booth peeped into the studio and stared at the couple seated in two comfortable chairs. "Johnson and Loretta, your segment will start once the Airtel commercial is over."

They looked at her and nodded. Johnson wore his signature black suit. Beside him, Loretta looked stunning in her blue pinstripe skirt and blouse.

"Louisa, you will start in 30 seconds," the woman said to a lady in a stylish dress who would anchor today's Johnretta interview segment.

"Thank you, Chioma," Louisa said.

For the past two weeks, Johnson and Loretta had been preparing for the wedding. They had hired food caterers and had started working with a popular wedding planner, getting the best of everything. The bridegroom's Tuxedo had been shipped from London, and Loretta had paid a fellow fashion designer to work on her own bridal dress. Now, her unique wedding gown was almost ready.

They would shut down the city next week Saturday, no doubt. For the past two weeks, they appeared on TV programs, honouring interviews and taking photographs with celebrities and journalists. Right now, *Johnretta* was the new internet sensation in the country. Fans were talking about the wedding on Twitter, Facebook, and Instagram. Most fans were still debating Loretta's diamond ring's worth, and this afternoon, they were in the studio of Starlight TV for an interview.

"Alright, Airtel Commercial is over," a voice from the control booth said. "We will begin in three, two, one…"

The monitor flashed to the round room where Louisa, the program anchor, and the couple sat.

"Hello viewers," Louisa started, flashing her signature smile. "With me are the latest couple in town—Johnson and Loretta, whose upcoming wedding is billed to shut down the city. They are here with me to share their love story with us." She fixed her gaze at the couple. "Let me start with the question Johnretta fans want to know, how did you meet each other?"

Loretta flashed her perfect smile, which revealed her dimples and white teeth to the camera. "Well, my friend dragged me to a party one evening. One hour into the party, I was in a bad mood and had begun to regret ever coming to the party. So, I went to the bar to drink away my sorrows and then go home. Then, just like a knight in shining armour, he appeared, joined me in the bar and lightened my mood." Loretta rested her head on Johnson's shoulder, and he brushed the strands of her hair which covered her right ear with his hands.

Louisa grinned. "Hmmm, this is so romantic. I can't wait to get married too."

The couple smiled back.

"There is news that your wedding is coming up next Saturday. How is the preparation for the wedding? Everything about your upcoming wedding is trending on social media. You've made quite many fans who identify themselves as Johnrettans."

Johnson nodded and said, "We are grateful that we have gotten so much support from our fans. I'm glad to have the support of my friends in the real estate industry. Some called and introduced us to the best wedding planners that would take care of different aspects of the wedding and its reception. We are definitely not settling for less."

Louisa looked at her notes and glanced at them. "Is it true you will spend your honeymoon in Paris?"

Johnson held Loretta's hands and said, "No, we will go to Santorini."

Louisa shot him a curious glance. "Never heard of it. Where is it?"

Johnson said, "It's a small island in Greece known for its sparkling sunsets and pristine whitewashed villas. It's a lovely place to create beautiful memories."

"And make babies," Loretta interjected. Johnson pulled her close and kissed her on the forehead.

Louisa stared at them in wonder. "Your love story moved so fast," she resumed. "You met barely a month ago, and now you are getting married. I am fascinated by your pre-wedding pictures, which I saw on Social media. Just looking at you right now, there is no doubt that both of you look perfect for each other."

"You got it right," Loretta said, "Sometimes in life, you can be with a person for years and feel something is missing. And then, you meet the one that connects with your soul and everything clicks right away. This is the summary of our love story." Loretta rested her head back on Johnson's shoulder.

Johnson expression beamed. "Every new day is a blessing. It was our hearts that made the choice."

***

At the same time the Starlight TV interview was going on, Ray arrived in the detention room after Oliver called him.

For the past two weeks, he had been to night clubs and motels interviewing several people. Still, no one knew anything about the Dragon Cartel. In his heart, he knew some of them were afraid to talk. There were rumours of a dangerous gang with a death squad operating in the city, but there was no evidence. And worse, Breya stuck to his story. He kept claiming innocence and had finally gotten a lawyer. This was what Ray hated about the system. Breya might even escape the wrath of justice at the end, and the case would be one of the hundreds of unresolved files.

Oliver had called him into his office five minutes earlier. He mentioned that Breya's lawyer wanted to talk to him.

Ray entered the cell and met with Breya's lawyer, Pius Okoro, a criminal lawyer known for his cunning and devious character streak. Law enforcement agents hated Pius. He had a perfect record and had never lost in a court case.

"What is it, Pius?" Ray didn't have any time to waste.

Breya was still under handcuff.

"My client wants to talk to you," Pius said.

Ray glanced at Breya. Breya looked older than his age and had lost ten pounds since he was put in detention.

"I can tell you everything you need to know. This shit will soon get ugly. I'm serious," Breya said.

Ray became alert. "I'm all ears. How long have you been working for the Dragon cartel? Where are these criminals?"

"Yes, I admit I worked for the cartel," Breya started, his expression revealing he had been preparing for this.

Ray felt the adrenaline pumping through his bloodstream. *This is it. It is coming. Finally.*

"What was my motive for doing this?" Breya smirked. "Isn't it that obvious? The money is good. It is better than the crap we are paid here."

His words were like a punch to Ray's face. He kept his cool. "How do you communicate with them? Who were you sending those messages?" he asked.

Breya grinned and glanced at Ray. "Smart agent. I know you, Ray. Don't be too fast to climb the ladder. I know how this works." His expression tightened. "I want immunity. Get it for me, and I will tell you everything you need to know."

"No way. You don't get to decide the terms, Breya. You will rot in jail," Ray snapped and stormed out of the detention room. They had wasted his time.

CHAPTER TWENTY-SIX

The next week moved in a blur for Loretta and Johnson, at the backdrop of a media frenzy and a busy schedule. They quickened plans for the wedding, and Loretta found herself in constant phone calls attending to the tiniest details.

The couple's week was packed with activities. On Monday, they attended an event in David Attah's house which he held in Johnson's honour. On Tuesday, the couple were at Maitama with friends to open a new shopping mall built by Johnson's real estate company. On Thursday, they attended an award ceremony at the International Conference Centre, Abuja, where they were given an award as the Couple of the Year as voted by fans in an online poll. Loretta was recognized in the event for being an exceptional fashion designer.

On Friday, the eve of the wedding, Loretta met with the Pastor of House on the Rock Church, where they finalized plans for the wedding church service. Johnson made international calls with the receptionist of their chosen hotel in Santorini. The couple would leave for their honeymoon on Sunday morning, and Loretta couldn't wait to enjoy a one-month of honeymoon with her soon-to-be-husband.

It was mid-July, and the rainy season had turned trees in Abuja to green, giving the city's landscape a fresher look. The couple cancelled a bachelor party organized in their honour by their friends and all events they were supposed to attend on Friday evening. It had been a hectic week, and they wanted to have that evening for themselves.

Loretta lay on the bed with Johnson that evening. Warmth and happiness flushed through her as she opened her smartphone, scrolling through pictures of Santorini.

The scenery of their honeymoon location was cosy and mouth-watering. She couldn't wait to relax on the beach with Johnson with just a bikini and no care in the world. A smile warmed her face as she stared at the strong back of her man as he stood bare-chested outside the half-open door of their master bedroom, making a phone call.

Tomorrow would be their wedding day. She couldn't wait to say, 'I do.'

***

That Friday afternoon, as Ray was clearing his desk, he heard a knock on the door. He told the person to come in. The door opened, and a figure entered. Ray glanced up and beamed, his expression full of relief. It was Frank.

"Frank, it's nice to see you again," he said as he came off his desk and hugged his partner lightly. "Aren't you supposed to be recovering at home?"

Frank grinned. "I'm back, Ray. I can't just be relaxing on my couch while knowing that people's lives are in danger because these criminals are still out there. I will never forgive myself."

Ray stepped back and studied him. "You feel better now?" He observed he had recovered but was worried that he still walked with a slight limp.

Frank smiled. "Thanks for your concern, partner. Look at me now. I'm as fit as Cristiano Ronaldo."

Both men chuckled. Frank left afterwards, and Ray went back and finished clearing the files on his desk. Next, he wrote a report he would give to his boss.

In the evening, Breya finally agreed to talk after a brutal one-week interrogation session. Ray was in the cell with Oliver and some senior agents when Pius convinced Breya to speak in exchange for just seven years in prison. Ray was sure Pius wanted to wriggle his client out of this one. But Breya committed treason, and he didn't have much room for manoeuvre.

Feeling desperate and running out of time, Breya wanted to use his lawyer to reveal his detention to the press. The agency threatened to deny him access to a lawyer in retaliation. In the end, he had no other option but to listen to his lawyer and agree to a reduced sentence. Once Breya signed the documents, he decided to tell the agency what he knew.

Ray, Ezekiel, Frank and three senior agents were in the detention room when he began to spill the beans, with shock registered on their faces.

"The Dragon Cartel is actually made up of two different criminal gangs," Breya said, blood dripping from his face.

"Two different gangs? Have they always been like this?" Ray asked as he stood beside Oliver.

"They split off a year ago over a disagreement about how the cartel should operate. I do not know the specifics."

"How did you know this?" Ray asked.

"I figured this out when I noticed a change in the way they communicate with me. Nine months ago, a man with a different name started communicating with me and told me to stop giving information to Mai Hikima."

Ray raised his eyebrow. "Who is Mai Hikima?" What are the names of people that communicate with you?"

"I don't know their real names. They use aliases and code names. I never got to know their real identity. Mai Hikima was the contact I had been working with for the first two years I worked with them. It is a Hausa word which means the wise one."

"How do the cartel pump the drugs into the city? Do they have prostitution rings here in Abuja?" Ezekiel asked.

"They use street dealers. That is all I know."

Silence encroached the room.

"There is something you need to know," Breya said.

Ray edged closer to the table. "Go on."

"Something else is going on. I observed it recently. The group I'm working with are planning something. I don't know what it is. But I know it's not good news."

Ray looked him in the eye and said, "We need to stop them, Breya. Do you have any vital information that can help us?"

"Find a man named Raze Brown. This may also be an alias. But whoever he is, he is the key to this puzzle," Breya muttered.

"Raze Brown, the club owner who is missing?" Ray asked.

"Yes, he's bad news."

"And there is one more thing."

"What is it?"

"They are holding some women as hostages. Those women don't know it yet. Most of them believe they would be taken to Europe where they would get a better life. These are women they ship out there and force to become prostitutes."

Ezekiel heard this and said, "Where are they holding these women?"

"I don't know," Breya said.

CHAPTER TWENTY-SEVEN

Wuse District, Abuja
9:30 a.m.

The gold-plated Limousine climbed down from the hilly cobblestone avenue in Aminu Kano Crescent and entered the busy Ahmadu Bello Way. Attached to the vehicle was the inscription *'About to Wed.'*

The driver, Peter Mansour, swore under his breath as he reached a bend where they were held by a red traffic light. They were running late to House on the Rock Church, where the most talked-about wedding would occur. It had been trending for three weeks on Social Media. Many celebrities have announced on Twitter that they would cancel their engagements this Saturday to attend the wedding.

Anxiousness broke across Peter's face because of the traffic that had formed around them. Still, when he stared through the driver's glass and saw the calm expression on the faces of the two occupants in the passenger's seat, he relaxed. A minute later, the red light changed to green, and he heaved a sigh of relief and pressed down hard on the throttle.

The dark-complexioned David Attah dressed in a black London suit and the light-skinned man in a stylish black tuxedo beside him were having a light conversation in the back. David whispered something in the other man's ear, and they broke into laughter. David looked at his friend's face and discovered he was sweating despite the cold air inside the vehicle. He removed the white handkerchief from his friend's breast pocket and used it to wipe the sweat off his face.

"Johnson, how did you do it? I still can't believe that you are finally getting married."

A gentle smile softened Johnson Omata's aristocratic facial features. The words of his best man were like music to his ears. He lifted his right hand, stared at his Rolex watch, and relaxed back on the soft leather chair. They would reach the church premises in twenty minutes. His fiancée's white limousine was two minutes ahead of theirs. *His Loretta.* His eyes flashed with happiness, and for the first time in his life, he felt the peace that had eluded him for years. It was as if his life had been heading to this very moment when he would finally achieve his life-long goal of marrying the woman of his dreams. He rested his hands on his laps as the light from his $2 million diamond ring reflected against the side window.

Everything about him, from the imposing physique, his perfectly carved beard, to his black, polished, custom-made shoe whispered new money. At the age of 35, Johnson was one of Africa's youngest millionaire entrepreneurs. Last year, he appeared on Forbes, CNN, and Time Magazine, where he was recognized for his grass-to-grace story and exceptional business acumen.

At the beginning of this year, an Abuja newspaper called 'Sensational' named him the Abuja Golden boy and one of the most eligible bachelors in the capital city. After investing over ₦ 500 million in real estate, setting up shopping malls and doing ₦ 200 million giveaway for 100 Nigerian youths on Twitter, Africa Business Magazine named him the African Young Entrepreneur of the Year.

Johnson felt destiny was aligning for him. Now that he was set to marry the breath-taking fashion designer, Loretta Olawale, he couldn't ask for more. At that moment, his phone began to ring, bringing him back from his reverie.

David looked on in curiosity as his friend brought out his Samsung phone from his pocket. Johnson stared at the number but didn't recognise it. He picked the call. "Hello," Silence. Before he could speak again, the call disconnected.

"Who is that?" David asked.

"I don't know." Confusion lined Johnson's face. Something was not right. He could feel it. As he was about to put the phone back in his pocket, his ringing tone shattered the silence in the car. He stared at the Caller ID. The same number. *Again*. He picked the call, and series of events happened all at once.

"Hello," he raised his phone this time.

"Johnson, it's about time," a deep voice bellowed at the other end of the line.

"What? Who is this? I—"

"Help me! Please!" A shrieking cry sounded in his ears. It was from a woman in severe pains. Johnson quickly recognized the voice and his heart raced. It was the voice of his wife-to-be, Loretta. How could this be? Panic settled on his face.

"Johnson, what is going on?" David was saying.

At that moment, the driver braked hard, the car screeched to a halt, forcing them to jam their faces against the front seat. The driver veered off from the main road and took a narrow route.

Alarm bells rang on Johnson's ears. "Peter, what are you doing?"

"Oga, I'm sorry that it has come to this. I have no choice."

"Johns—"

Suddenly, the side window shattered, and a bullet hit David on his forehead. He dropped dead instantly. Johnson quickly opened the passenger door beside him and jumped out of the vehicle, which was at a hilltop. His body rolled down violently until it hit a tree. His whole body ached with pain as he got up with incredible difficulty. He stumbled down the hill and dived inside the river beside him, his body dodging the enemy's bullets. A fairy-tale wedding had turned into a nightmare.

CHAPTER TWENTY-EIGHT

Loretta's white limousine was two minutes ahead of her fiancé's vehicle. Her expression was peaceful as she rested her back on the soft leather seat. The July sun was punishing, its reflection heating up the car. She had told the driver to turn off the air-conditioner. When he'd switched it on, and she began to feel cold. She was surrounded by Amanda, her chief bridesmaid and four ladies by her left who were her bridesmaids.

Amanda wiped off the sweat forming on her forehead, smearing a considerable part of her makeup. She attempted to touch the driver to put the AC back on, but Loretta held her arm and shook her head.

"We will soon get there, Loretta. This is your big day. Just relax," Amanda assured her.

Loretta tried to relax but couldn't. Her mind was going through a million details. Earlier this morning, she was on a phone call with the food caterer, the baker, the truck driver, the wedding planner, and the pastor, making sure everything was all set. This was where her perfectionist streak drove everyone around her crazy. One of them told her that she worried too much.

Her fiancé didn't care about all these details, which fell on her shoulders. But she was not bothered, wanting the day to be perfect.

This is your day, Loretta. Be happy. No more worries. She did the usual thing that made her smile. She closed her eyes and imagined how beautiful her life with Johnson would look like. She was glad that she had gotten her own prince. The king of her heart. She couldn't wait to walk across the aisle and say the eternal vows with him that would make forever come true.

A hand nudged at her. "Loretta, your phone." Amanda handed her the Samsung smartphone.

"What?" She stared at Amanda. Annoyance broke across her face. "I don't need any calls now. I thought I told you! I just need to relax for these few minutes."

"It's a message."

Loretta gave a deep sigh and clicked it open. "Where are you guys? Chuks and I are waiting at the church with other guests." The message came from Cynthia.

A smile appeared on Loretta's face. She texted back. "We are on our way."

The phone buzzed ten seconds later. "Babe, many dignitaries are here. This is going to be mind-blowing."

"Smiles," she typed and texted her back.

"I can't wait to see you in your exquisite wedding gown," the message from Cynthia read.

"Thank you, babe. See you soon," she checked her watch and resumed her typing, "in 18 minutes." She clicked send and gave the phone to Amanda.

At that moment, someone in the car said, "Look ahead. Some men with guns blocked the road. Look…"

The driver braked hard, and their head slammed against the leather chair.

One of the gunmen raised his weapon and fired. The front tire burst, and the vehicle lost control.

"Oh my God. Oh my God." Amanda screamed in a panicked voice.

The car careened off the road, slammed into a tree, killing the driver instantly. The girls were paralysed with shock. Loretta opened the passenger door and struggled to get out.

Someone was sobbing in the car. "My leg. My leg."

Loretta climbed out of the car and tried to help Amanda come out. Amanda winced in pain and cried out for her leg. Three of the girls came out from the other side of the car. Loretta used all her strength and dragged

Amanda out of the vehicle. The moment Amanda stood by the door, her mouth formed an 'O' as a red crimson appeared on her chest, and she fell.

"Amanda!" Loretta panicked, her eyes filled with terror.

Two gunmen appeared by her side and shot the rest of the bridesmaids to death. Loretta's eyes widened. For a long moment, her head spun. Rough hands dragged her to a black sedan by the roadside.

"Leave me alone," she yelled.

As they reached the car, a man beside her made a call and disconnected it. He redialled the number and put the phone on speaker. He said some words Loretta couldn't hear. "What? Who is this? I..." a voice at the other end of the line said.

"Help me! Please!" Loretta screamed for whoever was out there to hear.

In the flash of a second, a black cloth was slipped over her head. Her hands were tied, and as she made to scream again, one of the gunmen put a piece of rag in her mouth, wedging it between her teeth. Rough hands pushed her inside the car. The gunmen entered quickly, and the car lurched violently forward. Everything happened in less than two minutes.

Loretta didn't know how long they were on the road. After what seemed like a long time, the vehicle stopped, and she was dragged out of the car. A huge man carried her on his shoulders, and she kicked and pushed to no avail. He dropped her inside a room and removed the black cloth that covered her face. As a stream of light rushed into her eyes, she observed the room had thick walls and tiny windows.

She trembled as a shiver ran through her. Her wedding gown was torn and dirty, just as her life had become in such a short time. Right on her wedding day. She couldn't believe that this was happening.

"Please, don't hurt me," her voice came out as a pitiful plea. "I will give you money, anything you want. Today is my wedding day. Please, let me go."

But no one listened to her. If they did, it fell on deaf ears. The front door slammed in front of her, and she heard departing footsteps.

CHAPTER TWENTY-NINE

Johnson swam through the river as the bullets raged on. His mind was in a million places as he thought about the irreversible damage this would do to everything. He managed to block the thoughts and lock them at the bottom of his mind.

Right now, the only thing that mattered was survival. His mind scanned through many options as he considered different means of escape and discarded them quickly. He kicked his legs and swung his arms fast, and his head soon bounced on the surface.

A bullet rang behind him, splitting bubbles of water into hundred tiny pieces. He dived deeper inside and followed the river channel, swimming for fifteen minutes until the water became shallow. When his head popped out from the water, his eyes swept across his surrounding, but he didn't see anyone. The vast empty land surrounding the shore stretched for a long distance.

He tried to move but groaned as the pain on his shoulder shot across his body. He had been shot. Perhaps when he dived into the river. This can't be happening on my wedding day, he thought as memories of the attack played like a horror movie in his mind. His wedding guests, including A-list VIPs—celebrities, top government officials and business moguls, were waiting for him and his bride at House on the Rock Church. The church service was supposed to have started by now.

"Help me please!" The shrill female voice echoed in his mind, making him almost lose control of his emotions. They had taken Loretta. His pulse raced, and he regretted not bringing the police to escort them to the

wedding. Shit. And David—his best friend had been killed. He blinked as sadness swept across his face.

He couldn't imagine what they'd done to his bride and the people in the vehicle with her. Peter had sold him to the enemy. How did they get to him? How much did they give him? Did they threaten his family? This was a mess. His well-crafted life had been blown apart.

He knew who ordered this hit on him: Raze Brown, the head of the Dragon Cartel.

So, the man was still alive, which meant Duru—Johnson's right-hand man—whom he sent along with some of the men loyal to him to kill Raze had lied to him.

Duru had returned three weeks ago injured with a bullet on his shoulder without the rest of his team. He had told Johnson a long story of how the team engaged Raze and his men in a violent shootout. In the end, he and Raze became the last men standing. But Duru got lucky and took him out before Raze could pull the trigger.

Does this mean Duru had been lying to me all along?

Johnson's mind was hazy. His face tightened, and he winced in pain. There were so many unanswered questions. He couldn't think clearly right now. He thought he'd removed all the obstacles on his path before the wedding, but now he knew that he underestimated Raze Brown.

Loretta. He shut his eyes and flipped them open. He couldn't imagine the pain his bride would be going through right now.

They should not touch the love of my life.

She was the only one he opened his heart to. Now, they had taken her away from him at the worst possible time. Did they do this to punish him? Or was it as revenge from Raze Brown?

First, he had to find out what went wrong and find a way to rescue her. There was no one he could trust right now. How would he know which of his men were still loyal to him? It was hard for him to believe this was his wedding day. His hands trembled, and he clenched his fists. He summoned the last of his strength and rose from the wet sand. His eyes darted right and left, and he ran.

***

By eleven in the morning, Ray drove to his house to drop a stack of files he wanted to study when he returned in the evening. As he closed his door after dropping them and headed to his car, his phone jangled, and he picked the call.

"Ray, it's Frank. Please, come to Ahmadu Bello Way."

His body rang with alarm. "What happened?"

"There was a shooting involving murder and possible kidnapping of a couple going to the church for their wedding."

Ray's heart skipped a beat. "I'm on my way."

He ran to his car and drove right through the gate, onto the busy road. He increased the speed as cars and landscapes blurred around him.

Within fifteen minutes, he reached the crime scene. He had seen a small crowd at a narrow road beside the Ahmadu Bello highway. He followed the road and stopped close to the crime scene. As he stepped out from his car, the July sun bore into his face in a rage forcing him to blink several times as his vision adapted to his surroundings.

Frank saw him and started walking towards him. The place was flooded with DSS Agents, police cruisers, newsmen and cameramen. God, soon this place will turn into a media circus, Ray thought.

When Frank reached where he was, he said, "What happened?"

"The couple were attacked on the way to their wedding," Frank replied.

"Shit."

Ray saw newsmen swarming close to a white limousine with shattered windows smeared with blood. He called a DSS agent and barked out orders. "Seal this place with a yellow tape. No one should go near it. This is a murder investigation. Work with the police to barricade this premise. Tell the newsmen to go back. We have no comment for now."

"Yes, sir."

Ray and Frank weaved their way through the crowd and reached where the Limousine sat. He greeted two policemen, flashed his Cred, and peeped through the shattered window of the white limousine. His mouth went dry when he saw the disturbing scene. Blood spread across the leather seat of the car, some smearing at the window. A man in a black suit lay sprawled across the passenger seat with a hole on his head.

"Who is this?"

"His name is David Attah. He was the best man," said Frank.

"Is that from a nine millimetre?" Ray asked, observing the bullet wound.

"Yes, he was killed by a bullet from an auto rifle."

Ray's eyes swept across the driver's seat. A man on a black coat rested on the steering. Blood dripped from the corners of his mouth. There were two bullet holes on his back.

"This is Peter Mansour, the driver. We discovered a few minutes ago that he worked for the bridegroom," Frank explained.

Ray stared at the two bodies for a moment longer. "Were the couple together in the same vehicle?"

"No."

"Where is the bride's vehicle?"

"It's three minutes ahead."

"Let's go," Ray said.

They entered Ray's Camry. Ray reversed the vehicle and soon entered Ahmadu Bello road. He drove slowly along the highway and stopped when they saw another white limousine surrounded by a small crowd. Both men climbed out once Ray parked the car by the roadside.

They flashed their Creds and forced the crowd to create a red-sea line. Ray gasped when he approached the vehicle. The scene he met was sickening. Blood splattered on all the windows of the car. There were six dead bodies. Five of them were in a pink gown. The sixth was the driver, who wore a brown suit.

"Who are they?" Ray asked.

"The five ladies are the bridesmaids. The girl in the centre appeared to be the chief bridesmaid. The man is their driver." Frank responded.

Ray's gaze swept through the car. Afterwards, he and Frank stepped away. "This is a professional hit. This couple was about to get married. Why would anyone want to kill them?"

"We found something else," a voice yelled.

They rushed to where the officer was. A DSS agent came out with a card and gave it to Ray. Ray and Frank stared at it. It had a message written in bad handwriting. "This is not over yet. Come and get her." At the right-hand-side of the card was the head of a dragon.

"It's the dragon cartel," Frank said.

Ray nodded slowly, its dangerous implication becoming clear in his mind. As he considered it, confusion lined his face. "This message was sent to someone. Who is missing here?"

"Yes, we figured the hit was ordered on the bride-groom. We didn't find his body. We figured he escaped.

The person they referred to must be his bride. Her body is not here as well."

Ray narrowed his eyes. "What is the name of the bridegroom?"

"Johnson Omata. I discovered he is quite popular."

Recognition poured into Ray's mind. He had heard the name somewhere. Perhaps on TV. "What is the name of the bride?"

"Loretta Olawale."

Ray heard the name and stiffened. "Come again. Please."

Frank shot him a curious glance. "Loretta Adewale Olawale." This time, he made sure to call her full name. "You know her?"

Yes, he knew her. She was the love of his life, still was. His head ached with a burning headache. He couldn't block the pain which broke through the surface of his mind carrying long-held memories. Memories of her. Memories of them together. Memories of the pain. They were all mixed up, flashing fast in a way that almost drove him crazy. This case had helped him to move on from a painful heartbreak. Now, this tragedy had brought him back right where he started—getting them together in the same case in the worst possible way. His heart pounded.

Loretta, what the hell have you gotten yourself into? He had to rescue her and unravel what else was happening here.

CHAPTER THIRTY

The girl opened her mouth and allowed the huge dick to slide all the way to her throat. She moved her tongue up and down the length and went all in. She pulled her head out a minute later, coming up for air. She was sitting on a chair beside a heavily tattooed man with large forearms of non-descript age. The man sat behind a massive desk in a vast room filled with wine and alcohol cellar. A big dog named Black Mamba sat close to his seat while wiggling its tail.

The girl dove in again, and the man let out a groan as he caressed her long hair with his thick fingers. He pulled out a pipe from the desk, lighted it, inhaled for a long moment and blew out a cloud of smoke. The room smelt of stale air. The girl pulled out and lapped her tongue across the tip. He lost control and exploded. She opened her mouth for him, and he fired the hot liquid in her mouth.

At that moment, the door opened, and two men came in. Raze Brown touched the girl and whispered in her ear. She wiped her face and left the room. Raze zipped his trouser and straightened his clothes. Time for business. He flashed his furious gaze at the two men. *This better be good.*

Raze Brown was a heavily built man with a big beard and an intimidating presence. He was still furious that his informant in DSS had been caught. The man was not an ordinary informant. He was the team leader of the unit investigating his cartel. Over the years, the agent had given them credible intel that has helped them stay ahead of the DSS.

Now, no one was telling him anything. What was he going to do? Silence the informant to keep him from revealing the truth? He might have talked already. This was how the world worked. That piece of shit would talk when given just a little shove. All these were happening less than a year when his own right-hand man pulled the carpet beneath his feet. Well, he intended to even the score right away.

He took another drag from the pipe and lifted his head, sending the smoke billowing to the ceiling. He dropped it on the table and turned to face them.

"What?" he spat out.

"Boss, he escaped," the lead man said, his legs unsteady on the tiled floor.

Raze glared at him as rage crawled up his spine. He picked the gun on his desk and pulled the trigger. The man grunted and fell on the ground, his eyes wide open.

"What about the girl?" he asked the second man.

"We...have...her," he stuttered.

"Bring her here."

"Yes, sir."

***

Loretta's hands trembled as she sat on the hard, bare floor inside a room in the middle of nowhere. The time from when she was kidnapped until now had been pure terror.

No, this can't be happening, she thought as tears pooled at the corner of her eyes. But she couldn't sob anymore because she had been crying for a long time.

Oh my God, where was Johnson, the love of her life? What had they done to him? Had they killed him? Who are these people? What do they want? Why today of all day? Her mind was fuzzy, searching for answers to questions she didn't understand.

Guests would be waiting for them at the church—friends from the fashion industry, Cynthia and her husband, Chuks, who had been so happy for her, celebrities, and TV crews. They would all be distraught right now. Johnson's mother would be worried to death.

The attack on the road had shattered her life. Images of Amanda and the bridesmaids who were killed by the gunmen flashed through her mind, and she let out a shrill cry. Her head spun. Her world was falling apart, and she couldn't make it stop. Worse, she had no answer for why any of this was happening. There were no signs, no warning.

She didn't know how long she had been here or where this place was. Was she still in Abuja? Was she still inside the country? At that moment, a hand slid a plate of jollof rice and a water bottle through the door. She ignored the food and water. Her body was numb with shock, and she did not have an appetite. She lay on her back to rest but couldn't. Her mind was restless. She kept seeing images of the shooting in her mind.

Ten minutes later, the door opened, and two men with tattooed arms entered. One of them dragged her up. They led her through a long, winding hallway that zigzagged thrice and opened at a straight road leading to the front door. They advanced across a large open field and headed to a one storey building in the vast area.

Loretta surveyed the place and blinked hard twice. What was this place? A farm? A Barn? They had just stepped out of a large building and were heading to a much smaller house. Her eyes darted left across the open space, and she saw farmland with maize, flowers, and vegetables. At the far end was a well-constructed piece of wood supporting an overhead tank.

"Where are we going?" Her voice was weak and tinged with fear.

"It's time for you to see the boss," the man holding her hand replied.

CHAPTER THIRTY-ONE

The moment Ray left the scene of the shooting, he arranged to meet with Mrs Cynthia Udoh, who had left the wedding venue and gone back to her house with her husband. Frank went ahead to question Johnson Omata's mother. They had gotten information that Caroline Omata was still at the House on the Rock church where she came to attend her son's wedding.

Ray arrived at the apartment building where the couple lived by 11 am and parked the car outside the gate. The couple had moved to a new three-bedroom flat in a gated five-storey residential building in Garki Area 2.

Ray got out of his car, opened the gate, and advanced with purposeful strides. The residential building was imposing and was painted off-white. Two cars covered in black tarpaulin sat close to the wall of the fence. As he walked, two children stared at him from a balcony on the first floor. Someone directed him to the couple's flat, and he climbed upstairs to the second floor and buzzed the door the moment he reached their flat.

He heard footsteps and the sound of the door being unlocked. The door opened, and he came face to face with Chuks. They shook hands, and Chuks led the way inside. The sight made Ray stop for a moment. Cynthia was sobbing silently on the couch. Chuks rushed to her side to comfort her. She appeared to have been crying since they came back from the church. Seeing her seated on the couch opened a floodgate of memories, but he schooled himself to focus on the job at hand.

He was still standing when Chuks said, "Welcome, Ray. Please, sit."

Ray nodded and sat on a chair beside him.

"Can we get you a drink?" Chuks asked.

"Just water. Thank you."

Chuks yelled out a name, and a boy of eleven years popped his head into the living room. Chuks mouthed orders, and the boy rushed inside and came back a few seconds later with a bottle of water. He placed it on a small table next to Ray, greeted everyone and departed from the living room.

Ray took a sip and his eyes swept across the room. Three comfortable chairs stood at different sides of the room. The wall was covered with framed photographs of the couple's wedding. The volume of the flat-screen television resting on a TV stand was muted. He observed that they were watching a program on TVC News before he arrived. Ray didn't know how to proceed, especially while Cynthia sat there, shedding tears. He had known her as Loretta's best friend from their days in the university. But he never got along with her.

Cynthia dabbed her watery face with a white handkerchief. Ray looked in her direction, their eyes met, and she flashed him a nervous smile.

"Cynthia, I'm sorry for coming at this time. I know both of you are close. I am trying to do all I can to get to the root of this. This is why I need your help."

Cynthia nodded slowly.

"The information we have is that Loretta was kidnapped on her way to their wedding. Gunmen attacked her vehicle, shooting the driver and the bridesmaids dead. But we didn't find Loretta's body."

The moment Ray said this, more tears appeared in her eyes and wetted her cheeks.

"The same thing happened to the groom's vehicle. His driver and best man were killed in cold blood. We have no idea where he is. We assume that Loretta has been kidnapped. Johnson may have escaped during the shooting." Ray stared at Cynthia. "When was the last time you saw your friend, Loretta?"

"Just this morning, around seven, I came to their hotel room where they had booked the whole third floor. A make-up artist was with her, putting eyeliner and foundation on her face. The whole place was a flurry of activity. She was getting ready for her wedding. She looked so happy and peaceful, the perfect bride..." Cynthia's voice trailed off.

She regained her composure and continued. "I wished her well and told her we would be waiting for her at the church. We were in the church when one of the guests ran inside and told us about the shooting. He said he saw a car with shattered windows on the road as he came to the church for the wedding. Now, it's all over the news. I still can't wrap my head around this. Why will anyone do this to them? Where is she? And where is Johnson? God, please, let them be alive." She choked up.

Ray said, "We have reasons to believe that her husband-to-be is working with a drug cartel. The couple was caught in the middle of a gang war."

Cynthia pressed her hand on her chest. "Oh my God. You mean Johnson has a hand in this?"

Chuks said, "You mean this guy is a criminal? I felt something was off about him. I thought the whole show-off was over the top."

Ray edited his words and said carefully, "This is still an ongoing investigation. I believe we will get a clearer picture as we make progress."

"Oh my God," Cynthia put a hand on her mouth. "I put her life in danger. Loretta, forgive me." She glanced at Ray. "I'm sorry, Ray."

Chuks stared at his wife and frowned. "Honey, mind what you say to him. You didn't do anything wrong."

Ray stared at her in puzzlement. "What do you mean?"

"I encouraged her," she blurted out. "I felt Johnson was a responsible guy. I knew both of you were dating and had just broken up then, but I encouraged her to give him a chance." Her voice was filled with regret.

Ray waved a dismissive hand at her. "I get it. I know you never liked me or the idea of me dating your best friend. Johnson is a popular guy and probably a smooth talker. Who wouldn't like him? You don't have to beat yourself up about it. We can never know everything about someone."

"Please help—"

Ray interjected. "That's the case I'm working on. It's now the priority of our agency. We will get to the root of this case. We will find her. If she is still alive, we will rescue her," he rose and dropped his card on the table at the centre of the living room. "If you remember anything that will help us in this investigation, no matter how insignificant it is, please don't hesitate to call me."

"I will," Cynthia responded.

Ray rose and said, "Cynthia do you have the contact of Loretta's secretary, Jane? I'll like to meet her after this."

"Yes, I do," Cynthia said and brought out her smartphone. She searched for the number and read out the digits.

Ray saved it on his phone. "Thank you," he said.

He shook hands with Chuks. He waved at Cynthia and left. As soon as he entered his car, he called Frank.

"How did it go?" Frank asked.

Ray filled him in. "How about yours?"

"She was hysterical. When I started, she began to sob. I didn't know what to make of that. I had to stop everything else I came to do and console her. She swore her son would never involve himself in a crime. She said he has enemies who are envious of his success."

"What else?"

"I stayed behind and talked to her when she had stopped crying and had finally calmed down."

"But."

"I think she is holding something back," Frank said.

"Where is she now?"

"She just left the church. It appears she wants to take a taxi."

"I see." Ray hung up and dialled a number. "Pete, where are you?"

"At the agency," the voice at the other end of the line said.

"Caroline Omata just left House on the Rock church. Take two agents. I want you guys to mount surveillance. Monitor every move she makes and report back to me."

"Yes, sir."

***

Ray set up a meeting with Jane. He called her, and she gave him her address at Apo. He arrived at her cramped one-room apartment thirty minutes later. Jane was still in the blue gown she wore for the wedding. She hesitated to greet Ray and meet his gaze but opened the door and offered him a seat. Ray introduced himself and told her he was working on the case. "Jane, right now, we are working on finding exactly what is going on. We will find Loretta, and to fast-track this, I need your help. When was the last time you talked with your madam?"

Jane finally met his gaze and said, "I met her three days ago. She came to the office and wanted to know the stage we were in a new project for clients. She had not been coming to work lately. She was mostly spending time with her fiancé. They granted a lot of interviews and attended lots of events which kept her busy."

Was she really in love with him? Knowing they spent so much time together made Ray feel pangs of jealousy.

But it quickly disappeared, and he focused his mind on the task at hand.

"Was that the last time you heard from her?"

Jane shook her head. "She called yesterday and asked if anyone left messages for her. She told me to attend to business calls and make sure no one disturbs her until after her honeymoon."

Ray's heart raced. "Her honeymoon? Where were they planning to spend their honeymoon?"

"Santorini in Greece."

Ray nodded slowly. Loretta and her husband-to-be had a lot of plans in place. The tragedy that struck shattered everything. He was determined to find out how Johnson Omata connected to all of this. Was he one of the leaders of Dragon Cartel? Or the leader of the splinter group? How did he fit into the so-called gang war going on in the cartel? It was apparent to Ray that Johnson's action had put Loretta's life at risk.

He greeted Jane and left her apartment. He entered his car and started the engine, and the vehicle pulled him back into the bright Saturday sun.

CHAPTER THIRTY-TWO

Johnson trekked for three kilometres before he reached a busy highway. His head throbbed with a headache, but he was determined to push on. He had a lot to do, and nothing could slow him down. It was clear he couldn't go to his house in Gwarinpa. He wouldn't know who would be lurking there waiting for him to pop up.

He took a taxi to the Baron hotel in the city. He kept a room there and had paid a year's rent in advance. The money he had in his pocket was wet. He pleaded with the driver to give him a few minutes. He rushed into the hotel lobby. No words were exchanged with the receptionist. The plump woman behind the counter knew him, and as she gave him his keys, she eyed him with suspicion. *She knows.*

He wouldn't stay here long. She might call the police on him. Again, Raze Brown's men were also looking for him. No one in the cartel knew about this place, but he had to be careful. As he walked to his room, he made sure no one was following him. He entered his room, got a debit card, and used it to withdraw a bundle of Naira notes from the ATM in front of the hotel. He gave the driver a huge tip and rushed back to his room.

The next thing he did was to check the bullet wound on his left arm. Luckily for him, no bullet lodged in his body, and the injury was not deep. For the next four minutes, he cleaned the wound with a first aid kit in his room and covered it neatly with a bandage. He showered and quickly put on a black jacket and jeans. As he stepped out of the hotel, he called and rented a grey Sienna and drove for one hour to Kwamba in Suleja.

Suleja was a city north of Abuja. The city shared proximity with Abuja even though it was in neighbouring Niger State. Johnson parked the Sienna in front of a small apartment he owned. It was shielded from view by tall buildings which surrounded it like guards and offered him the privacy he needed to come in and leave anytime he wanted. This apartment contained his other life the public knew nothing about—the life he planned to leave behind. He punched in some numbers and set off his alarm at his security panel. He unlocked the door and switched on the light once he was inside the room.

Johnson advanced with stealth, walked past a tiny living room, and entered the bedroom. He pushed the bed on the floor aside, and the floor underneath revealed a square metal door. He opened the metal door and stared at the open box filled with credit cards, three international passports, a handgun, a burner phone, fake IDs, three hunting knives and auto rifles.

He was glad he had a backup plan. His goal had always been to plan for the best and the worst-case scenarios in everything. He switched on the burner phone and placed a call.

"Where are you?" he said to the person at the other end of the line.

"I heard the news. Sorry. Boss, who did this? We will hit them—"

"Skip it. Where?"

"At the location."

"Get the men ready. We have been compromised. Raze Brown. He found out and attacked."

"Shit."

"And they took my lady."

"This doesn't look good."

"The whole thing is already in the news, but that's the last thing on my mind right now. Get the men ready.

I will soon come and pick you guys up. But I want to be sure of the loyalty of the men I'm working with."

"We are at your service, boss."

"Once I say it's time, we'll move."

"Yes, sir."

He hung up and put the credit cards and burner phone inside the inner pocket of his jacket. He placed the hunting knife and handgun inside the belt area of his trouser. He put the dismantled auto rifles and their magazine inside a small black bag and left the apartment, locking the door on his way out. His headache returned as he imagined what Loretta would be going through right now. He felt something rise in him as he thought of what Raze and his men did to him and his bride. His hands gripped the steering wheel. *Give me more time, Loretta,* he pleaded in his mind as he kick-started the engine. The tires blew shards of dusk as the vehicle barrelled down the untarred road.

***

Raze saw Loretta being brought in through the door by two of his men and rose. He fixed his eyes on her, studying her with fascination as his meaty face brightened.

"Such a beauty. Johnson has eyes." He glanced at the man holding her. "It's okay, leave her alone. Let the princess relax. Today is her wedding day, remember," he said and chuckled.

The man nodded and stopped holding her. Loretta shivered and moved back until her body hit the wall. "Please, let me go. What do you want? Is it money? How much?" Her eyes were misty.

Raze studied her for a moment longer. It was clear that she was desperate to get away. She was like a caged bird whipping its wings in a hopeless battle to set itself free. "Don't be faster than your shadow, my lady. We have to follow due process."

"What?" Loretta asked, her face revealing pangs of frustration. Panic crept into her eyes as she managed to stare at him. "Where is Johnson? What have you done to him? Where is my fiancé?" She broke into a sob.

Raze cocked his eyes, and a cunning smile sprang across his face. "You don't know, do you?"

Loretta blinked in confusion.

"What do you know about Johnson?" Raze asked.

"He is my fiancé," she started. "He is an honest businessman who has done a lot of good for his country. He is a responsible man." Suddenly her eyes bore into his with defiance. "I can't say the same about you and your men whose hands are tainted with the blood of all the people you killed today." Tears were in her eyes, but her fear had vanished.

Raze detected anger in her voice. He was impressed. He clapped and broke into laughter. He stepped out of his seat, caressed his dog slightly and came in front of his desk, resting his bulky frame on the mahogany.

"Your husband is a killer. A criminal. A drug dealer." His hands tightened into fists. "He brought this upon himself."

Loretta froze. "No, it's not true. That's not Johnson. You've mistaken him for someone else. I know him. I know the man I fell in love with." She placed her arms across her chest.

Raze fixed his gaze on her. He approached her, and she pressed her back tightly against the wall. He cupped her jaw with his hand, feeling her body tremble. "Do you?" he asked as his anger boiled into a memory of heart-wrenching betrayal by a man he took as his younger brother.

As the head of Dragon Cartel, Raze was not afraid of law enforcement agents. But he was not stupid. He had been in the game for a long time to know how not to get burned.

His rule was simple. His men would keep pumping the drugs into the streets, but everyone would need to stay low as they made money. Don't flaunt the wealth—no need to attract unnecessary attention.

Johnson Omata was his second in command. His right-hand man. The heir to the throne. That was how close they were. Johnson knew the rules, but two years ago, Raze began to get reports that Johnson was disobeying the rules. He was building apartments and shopping malls and opening businesses. He was getting popular in the country and seemed to be enjoying his fame, forgetting who he was.

That was the worst thing about getting carried away, wasn't it? The first thing Raze did was confront him. Johnson didn't deny it. Raze could have killed him right away for breaking their code. But he had a soft spot for him. He had picked Johnson up from the streets of Ajegunle in Lagos when he was barely twenty. Lost and hungry, the younger man's life had been hopeless and without direction, his parents nowhere to be found. He put Johnson under his wings and watched him become good in the game.

He would later find out that Johnson's mother, unable to pay the bills and feed them both, had left him in the streets and got a job as a waitress at a restaurant. Such a heartless mother. Raze was shocked when she came back into his life—by then, Johnson was working under him. She apologized for her horrible behaviour, and he let her in. Poor Johnson, he couldn't even behave like a man and make her pay for what she did to him. Raze saw it all unfold, but he let it slide and watched him grow. After all, he had taken him as a brother. But what did Johnson do when he grew wings? He broke all his rules.

Raze had been visibly angry at Johnson and told him to end that life and embrace the life of the brotherhood.

He told Johnson he was putting the whole members of the cartel at risk by his foolish actions. Johnson had apologized and promised to change. Soon afterwards, he grew bolder and continued in his rebellious ways.

That was when Raze knew that Johnson had grown soft and foolish. A year ago, he finally decided to discipline Johnson. To his utter surprise, Johnson turned his back on him and the cartel. He pulled away from the cartel with men loyal to him and formed his own group. They had been at war ever since.

When Johnson broke away from the cartel, Raze had given new orders to his men. They were meant to slow down operations and tie off loose ends by killing anyone who disobeyed their demands, including any of the girls that planned to run away. That had been their policy for years in the cartel—no one broke the rule and lived to tell the story.

Because of Johnson's actions, he made it a priority. Thanks to the DSS informant, they had silenced all those who wanted to talk to the authorities. With that taken care of, he had focused his attention on Johnson and his group of bandits and making sure they'd regret their actions. But their skirmishes were nothing like the attack Johnson carried out against him three weeks ago, which was like striking a dagger into his heart.

He never knew Johnson was plotting to kill him. That night, he was at Flatlane, one of the clubs he managed and used as his cover. Ten minutes earlier, Raze had picked up a beautiful girl who seduced him with her swaying hips at the dancing floor. He took her to the back of the building for a quickie. He was plunging in through her back when the gunshots started. That had been his luck. He was startled but quickly pulled up his trousers. He told the girl to stay there and brought out his revolver, which he always had with him.

The men were on a shooting spree, and people in the club were running around in panic for safety. But the gunmen who wore masks were facing resistance from his men. He entered the building quietly and co-ordinated his men—those who had not been mowed down by bullets. His men overpowered the gunmen, taking out most of them. He became furious as adrenaline pumped through him. He shot down one of the intruders, and his men surrounded the last man who appeared to be their leader. His shoulder was bleeding. He raised his weapon and surrendered.

"Who are you?" Raze flashed his eyes at one of his men. "Remove his mask."

His men did as he ordered, and Raze's face fell and drained of blood. He recognized the gunman named Duru, a member of his cartel. The truth hit him hard on his chest. "Check all the slaughtered men. Remove their masks," he barked.

"Boss, they are our members." Someone shouted.

"I know these men. They are part of us," another yelled.

Raze's blood boiled. Who had the gut to do this? Who was behind this? He placed the muzzle of his gun at Duru's forehead. Duru's eyes flashed with panic.

"Tell me the truth right now, or I will blow your head off. Who sent you?"

Duru opened his mouth to speak and closed it. Raze pulled the trigger, and the bullet hit Duru on his shoulder. He cried out in pain.

"I will blow off your knees if you don't start talking. And you will never walk again."

Everyone, including Duru, knew that Raze was an unpredictable man given to fits of rage and violent outburst. No one messed with him.

"Johnson Omata," Duru let it out.

The moment Raze heard the words, the pain from the shock landed on his chest with a heavy thud. His heart constricted, but he quickly regained his composure.

As his mind and vision cleared, it dawned on him that he made a terrible mistake. He would have followed the cartel's policy and terminated Johnson and his men when they had pulled out months ago. This attack was an embarrassment of the highest order, meant to make him look weak in front of his men. He was determined to make things right.

But he decided not to send his men right away to Johnson's house and spray everywhere with bullets. He craved due process. A good strategy was better than a mere show of strength. He told Duru to rise. He told him part of the plan. Duru would spy on Johnson and report back to him.

"Go back. Tell Johnson that Raze Brown is dead. The injury on your shoulder will convince him that you fought hard and won but lost your men in the gun battle."

Duru accepted. He left and went to work, giving Raze daily reports that helped him study Johnson's routine. He then got information about Johnson's businesses and his wedding plans. Next, Raze put Johnson's driver, Peter, under his payroll. He paid Peter one million naira right away, and Peter's voice flashed with excitement the moment he called to confirm that he had received the money. Raze promised to pay him three million if he would give him information about his boss' wedding plans and the route they would take on the wedding day.

Peter had replied immediately. "That's easy, sir. Is that all?"

Raze smiled. "That's all, my new friend." He was satisfied with the way his plan was going.

The key to the whole plan was to wallop Johnson on his most vulnerable day, his wedding day. That was what he did. His goal was to capture them both and have his men bring them to him. Then he would look into both their eyes and put an end to their miserable lives with his gun. But Johnson got lucky and escaped. Was he lucky? He had captured his woman, and law enforcement agents who would be wondering why the attack happened were searching for him. But who would they ask?

Poor Peter, Raze thought as his mind came back to the present. He had given orders to his men to kill Peter and other passengers in both vehicles. Just tying up loose ends. He only wanted his men to bring the couple to him. But that was not how the plan went, right? Now the cartel had remained split into two. He still had most of the members by his side. Those who chose to be with Johnson were a small group of rebels. He would crush them all.

Ironically, Raze was enjoying this. He was just getting started. He went back to his desk and glanced at his men. "Send a message to Johnson. He has sixty minutes to be here. Let's finish this. Or she dies."

"Yes, sir."

CHAPTER THIRTY-THREE

Ray and Frank got the warrant to search each of Loretta and Johnson's apartments from the Abuja High Court. They both arrived at Loretta's two-bedroom apartment by twelve noon. Hot air blasted at their faces the moment they stepped out of the car. Frank worked on the lock, and both men entered the living room a minute later.

Loretta's apartment was like Ray remembered it. One of her towels was still on the couch. She must have been rushing to get everything ready for the wedding. A bottle of wine sat on a small table in the middle of the living room. Ray left Frank in the living room and entered her bedroom. Her make-up kits and skin lotions were still on the round table where she always kept them.

The room sparked memories in his mind. He remembered what happened the last time he was here. How Loretta had told him that she needed space and had broken up with him. Yes, she had told him she didn't have time for a relationship or marriage. But she had gone ahead to almost marry a man she met barely two months ago. That was odd.

He blocked the memories and swept his eyes across the room. His eyes caught an object under the bed. He knelt and brought it out. It was a bag. He unzipped it and brought out a red gown which was still attractively packaged inside black nylon. He read the words written in a small white paper placed inside it. *For you, my queen. – J.O.* A gift from Johnson Omata. She hadn't yet opened it. Perhaps, she kept it here and wanted to get back to it after the wedding.

Ray rose and met Frank the moment he stepped out of the room. "Did you find anything useful?"

"Nothing. She has been preparing for the wedding. It's clear she didn't know anything like this would happen," Frank said.

Ray nodded in agreement. They left the apartment and reached Johnson's house in Gwarinpa by one in the afternoon.

Ray observed as Frank gasped when their vehicle stopped in front of Johnson's plush residence. Johnson lived in the famous Gwarinpa estate. Ray thought he wouldn't be surprised when he reached his house, but now he was here, he was stunned as well.

"My God, this place is like..." Frank's voice trailed off as he tried to find the right words.

"A senator's house, yes, I thought as much," Ray said.

They flashed their ID and explained their mission to the gateman. The gateman nodded, rolled the big gate, and they entered. Both men stared in wonder as they strode across the parquet tiles that covered the compound. They couldn't take their eyes off the garden at the centre of the premises and the enormous swimming pool beside the house. The gatemen used a remote button and unlocked the glass door at the front of the building. They stepped in and took the long hallway, passing through a French door that led to the living room.

The living room was immaculate and smelt of new money.

"This man loves luxury items," Frank observed as they stared at the expensive Italian chairs. Ray took the rose flower vase that sat atop a small glass table. He peeped inside, but there was nothing out of place there. For the next thirty minutes, they searched the entire house, but nothing could point them to the double lives they suspected Johnson was living. If he was a criminal or drug dealer, there was nothing here to show it. No guns, no drugs, no clue. Anyone who came here would believe he was an honest businessman—a good citizen of his country.

It was clear to Ray that this was how he deceived Loretta. Most of his fans probably saw him as a saint, a generous man who could do no wrong. Johnson was successful in selling to the public the image of him he wanted them to believe. Now, looking around his well-organized house, Ray understood why anyone could easily believe him. His eyes caught piles of photographs on a study desk in his bedroom. But nothing was out of place. There were pictures of Johnson at different social events, receiving awards and a few of the couple together.

He tried to look closely to find out if what everyone said about the love the couple had for each other was true. Still, apart from the smile Johnson had for the crowd and the camera, Ray couldn't see anything else in his expression. Loretta's expression was complex for him to read. It was clear that both loved being together in public.

Ten minutes later, Ray gave up and was about to leave when Frank called his name from the living room. He raced to the room and saw Frank holding a framed photograph of Johnson's mother in his left hand. Frank had a white card in his right hand.

"The card was placed inside the framed photograph. The frame had broken into two, and the card was there," Frank explained.

Ray approached and stared at the photograph. It was a picture of Caroline Omata in her early thirties. She looked skinny and malnourished in the yellow apron she wore that one would wonder what was going on. The photo was taken outside a restaurant, probably where she worked at the time.

It was difficult for Ray to reconcile this picture with the plump figure of Caroline Omata he had seen in recent photographs.

"Something about the picture caught my attention, and I decided to take a look," Frank said and gave him the card. Ray stared at it and frowned.

09-UNIABJ-AN

The words were written with a black pen. It made no sense.

"I thought so too," Frank said, reading Ray's mind. "I didn't understand any of it."

Ray gave him the card and made to leave when an idea hit him.

"Give it back to me, please."

Frank obliged.

Ray collected the card and stared at it again. This time, he took his time. "09 is the area code of Abuja."

Frank glanced at him in surprise, wondering what he was getting at. "Yes."

"UNIABJ is University of Abuja."

Frank's expression brightened. "Yes, how could I have missed that?"

Ray stared at the card again. "What is AN?"

He waited for Frank to answer, but his colleague's face came up blank.

"That, I don't know." Frank paused and continued. "What's going on at the University of Abuja, and how is it connected to this case? He must have a reason for putting this card here."

Ray thought about it as his resolve became firm. "We will find out." He dialled a number. "Pete, tell three agents to meet us at Mabushi roundabout. We are going to the University of Abuja now."

"Yes, sir. On it," said the voice at the other end of the line.

***

Johnson met three of his men at Madalla, a small town in Suleja. When he saw them by the side of the road where Luka told him they would be, he slowed the vehicle and killed the engine. He looked through the window and studied Luka and the two barrel-chested men he came with. He knew Caleb and Ugo; they were part of the men who left Dragon Cartel to join him. They had stuck by his side even now everywhere was hot.

"Where is Duru?"

"His number is not going. I have not seen him for the past two days."

Johnson clenched his jaw. That sucker. He glanced at them. "Get in. We have no time," he yelled as he restarted the engine. Caleb and Ugo entered through the back passenger door, and Luka joined him in front.

"Tell others to standby and wait for my next instruction."

"Yes, sir," Luka replied.

"Boss, we must make sure they pay for every damage they have done."

Johnson frowned. Luka talked too much. He didn't need that right now. He needed to concentrate and focus on his plan. He waved at him to be quiet, and they drove in silence for the next thirty minutes.

They soon entered Umaru Musa Yar'Adua road. Johnson typed a text message on his phone and hit send. He dropped the phone and drove for another twenty minutes. The vehicle turned left, and as Johnson entered Mohammed Maccido road, his phone rang. He put it on speaker.

"Mai Hakimi, the boss said you have sixty minutes to be here, or she dies." His men heard the voice and stared at him knowingly. Luka gave his colleagues a sign that said, 'It's them', and they nodded. On hearing the threat, blood rushed to Johnson's face. "If you do anything…"

He heard a click which was followed by a chuckle, and his eyes flashed red. Raze Brown.

"Game over, tough guy. You think you are smart, right? It ends today. If you are not here in 60 minutes, I will start cutting her fingers and feeding them to my dog. I have purposely starved black mamba of breakfast and lunch."

Johnson's expression hardened. He fought the urge to lose control. "Let me speak to her."

"No, you have no power here. But let me play this beautiful music for you."

Johnson heard a shrill cry, and he became uncomfortable in his seat. *Loretta. What are they doing to her?* His knuckles tightened on the sterling.

"Boss," Luka wanted to say something, but Johnson eyeballed him to keep quiet.

"Raze, it's me you want, not her. Release her, let her go. This fight is between you and me. That girl is innocent."

"No," Raze snapped. "You don't get to dictate how this game plays. Here's my promise to you; before the end of today, both of you will be dead."

Johnson heard the click, which announced to him and his men that he had disconnected the call.

He restarted the engine and drove fast for five minutes, and soon entered a paved driveway that led to the University of Abuja's main campus's enormous gate. A security man opened the gate for him. Johnson brought out his hand and collected a driver's pass from him. The security man waved at him, and he smiled back and sped off across the tarred road.

CHAPTER THIRTY-FOUR

As Loretta was being taken back to the building where her room was, she saw five gunmen lined in front of the building. What was that about? Fear crept into her eyes, and a thousand questions flooded her mind. The two men entered the building, dropped her in her cell, and closed the door behind them. As Loretta sat on the bare hard floor, she couldn't stop replaying Raze Brown's words in her mind.

Johnson is a killer. He is a criminal. He is a drug dealer.

Her eyes brimmed with tears, and she shook her head. *No, it's not possible.* She remembered the beautiful memories they created together—the feel of his skin against hers—the beating of his heartbeat as she placed her hand on his chest. She remembered his deep, piercing eyes and the way he looked at her with desire and longing. Could those eyes have been hiding many secrets?

At that instant, a memory rushed through her mind, and her pulse raced. She remembered the day he made a call—she couldn't hear most of what he said, but she remembered the last two words he said. 'Do it." She remembered seeing his face harden. It was a side of him she had not seen before. But it had disappeared quickly before she could put much thought into it.

Sometimes, when he received a call, he would go to the bathroom, and she wouldn't hear what he was saying. God, she was getting paranoid. Had she been imagining all of these? Or was their relationship all a lie? A part of her told her Johnson couldn't have deceived her. He loved her. She saw it in his eyes—in the way he held her in his arms and protected her. His life was an open book. He had introduced her to his mum and to his friends at different events they attended together. He didn't live his life like a man who was hiding something from his fiancée.

But still, a painful thought lay at the back of her mind. It was obvious that this Raze Brown was furious at Johnson. He was a criminal, a gangster and had men who took orders from him. And right in front of her, he had called Johnson—her Johnson, and he had picked the call. She didn't hear his voice, but they had talked over the phone. She had listened as Raze ordered Johnson to be here within sixty minutes, or they would kill her.

How did Raze know Johnson? Were they business partners? What did Johnson do to Raze for him to want to kill them both? Was Johnson being set up by a friend or a business competitor who was envious of his success? Maybe they wanted to take him out of the way. Loretta's head hurt. She struggled to rein back the thoughts from her mind but failed. She didn't know what to believe. Worst, she didn't know what was going on.

At that moment, an uncontrollable sob tore out from her throat, and she let the tears fall as it became clear to her that this was worse than she thought. They were planning to kill her within the hour.

Ten minutes later, one of the men slipped in a bottle of water through the door, and she gulped it down quickly. She didn't see anyone for the next thirty minutes. Knowing they were planning to kill her, she now discovered that her life lay in her hands. A plan formed in her mind. Her heartbeat quickened. She thought about the risks and sucked in a deep breath. She had no other choice. She rose and stepped close to the door.

"Who is there?" she yelled.

Silence. No voice. No approaching footsteps.

"Please, I need to go to the restroom."

She called out for the next five minutes before a guard came and opened the door, holding a bunch of keys in his hand.

"What?" He flashed her a suspicious glance.

She told him. He looked sceptical but grudgingly told her to follow him. She followed him through the labyrinth of a passageway. The corridors were dark, and he had to make use of a torch. He stopped in front of a padlocked door marked B2. He used one of the keys and unlocked the padlock. "Enter. Be quick. This is not part of the orders they gave me. Next time, do it on the floor. And be fast. I'll wait outside."

She nodded. *It's now or never.* She made to enter the restroom but pushed him inside.

"What the hell?" he said in stunned surprise.

Loretta locked the padlock on the door fast and ran. The guard was inside and had the key, but she didn't mind.

Not knowing where she was going, she kept cutting right and left. She passed two sets of diesel generators and a jerrycan and entered a hallway that ended in front of a door marked B18. She turned the handle. It was unlocked. She opened the door and stepped in. Her eyes widened in astonishment at the scene playing in front of her. Young beautiful girls in their early twenties sat on a long rectangular table eating salad while chatting and laughing in low voices. Excitement glowed on their faces.

Travel bags sat on the floor beside the dining table. They looked at her with eyes bulging in shock.

What was going on here? A girl Loretta figured out was their lead girl approached her with a look of concern. "Who are you?" Her eyes took in Loretta's bizarre appearance.

Loretta became nervous as she felt a lot of eyes on her. She looked at her clothes and discovered why they were shocked at seeing her. She was still in her wedding dress. It was dirty and dusty. She looked like she came from the worst side of Ajegunle. "I'm a guest in the house," she muttered.

From her expression, Loretta knew the lead girl didn't believe her. She swept her eyes all over her in confusion. "Are you one of us?"

Who are you and what are you all doing here, she wanted to ask.

"No," she paused. An idea entered her mind, and she took the gamble. She stared at the lead girl as her face brightened. "It's possible I'm one of you. I'm still new here. A guard brought me here and left. Sorry. I'm not sure what to do next," she paused. "I see travel bags. Where are you going?"

The girl smiled. "I understand. The process can get quite confusing for newcomers," she paused, turned and glanced at the girls in the room. "The first group will travel to Italy. The group I belong to will be going to Dubai." Excitement shone on her face. "We are tired of staying in this country. No jobs. Hardship everywhere. The man that will take us abroad said we will get jobs easily over there."

Loretta found this hard to believe. They were all women. There was no man among them. These girls didn't know what else was going on here. They seemed to be living in a different world than the rest of everyone else in this hellhole.

"Who is this man you are talking about?"

The lead girl patter her shoulders. "You will like to join us, right? Wait here. He will soon be here. First, you need to change these dirty clothes."

Loretta didn't know if she was in the middle of another web of deception. It was evident that these girls didn't know who these men were.

CHAPTER THIRTY-FIVE

Johnson arrived in front of the old girls' hostel and cut the engine inside the spacious parking lot. The hostel was long, with more than five buildings that were strung together. Its front surrounding was an ample open space, tarred and neat. Young female students in shorts streamed in and out of the hostel's cafeteria.

It was the weekend, and the whole place was bursting with activity. A Mercedes Benz, three BMW and two black Toyota SUVs slid into the parking lot. Most of them were wealthy men who came to pick beautiful university girls for weekend relaxation. Some girls would often come back on Sunday evenings with loads of cash.

"Wait here," Johnson said to his men and stepped out of the car.

He texted her. "I'm here, baby."

The reply was quick. "Wow, finally. Give me a few minutes. I'm coming."

Satisfied, Johnson put his phone in his jacket pocket and waited. He had been dating Anna online for a year. They had met on Facebook, and their friendship had quickly blossomed into a relationship. They had not yet seen each other face to face. They had always fantasized on Zoom video calls about how they wouldn't wait to rip each other's clothes apart when they meet.

Anna was a final year student of Political Science. Thirty minutes ago, Johnson had texted her that he was coming to pick her up for a weekend getaway. They had been planning it for weeks, but Johnson kept postponing it—always telling her that something came up.

Johnson watched in awe as Anna stepped out of the door. She was what her picture promised—an ebony skin tone, big hips, lovely legs accentuated by tight jean trousers and a blue striped shirt. She saw him and recognition appeared on her face. She ran towards him and hugged him. He scooped her up and put her down, brushing his lips on hers just for a second, a promise of what their weekend held. Her eyes sparkled with desire, and her lips hung open.

"Finally," he said.

Her face brightened as she took a step back to observe him, her eyes eating him up. "You are so handsome. Wow, the pictures didn't do you justice." Her voice was soft like a Celine Dion's love song. Johnson was used to having this kind of effect on women. He'd heard this kind of compliment several times that it now bored him. But he put up a performance for her. He blushed. "You look stunning, my lady. Your shape is perfect."

Her smile lasted only for a few seconds. A frown appeared on her face, and she took another step back. "Isn't today your wedding day? I remember reading it somewhere on Facebook." Her eyes moved from him to the men in his car. "How come you are here, and who are these men with you?"

Johnson was not surprised. From their chats, he'd known that the twenty-two-year-old was very smart and intelligent. She was not a woman to be deceived or pushed around. She was just like her mother but also had her father's stubborn streak. He pointed at the men in his car. "Those men are my friends. About the wedding, I changed my mind."

"Why?" Curiosity shone in her eyes.

"I found out she was cheating on me with my best man."

Her face fell, and she looked at him with sympathetic eyes. "She lost a good man."

Johnson replied with a nod. He waited to hear the worst. She motioned with her hands for him to lead the way. He released a sigh of relief. He was glad she hadn't seen the news about the shooting yet, or she would have asked him about it. If he had arrived an hour longer, she would have seen it online.

Luka left the front door open and entered the passenger seat to allow Anna to stay with his boss at the front seat. She entered, and Johnson gently closed the door for her. Johnson observed she was in high spirit. He loved that. He entered through the driver's door, started the engine, and the vehicle zoomed off.

***

Ray drove into the University of Abuja's main campus just as Johnson's Sienna was leaving through the gate. Frank sat beside him at the front seat. The three uniformed DSS agents they picked from Mabushi round-about sat at the backseat. He parked beside the gate and met the burly security man who came to give him his driver's pass.

The man's face was set in a deep frown. Tight lines across his forehead showed he was a university employee who had worked under the sun for years.

As he approached them, his face bore a stern warning. "We don't park here. Either you go in, or you go out."

Ray alighted from the car and flashed his ID. He explained who they were and why they were there. The security man listened but said nothing. Other agents soon stepped out of the car and joined him. The blinding sun made one of the agents put on his dark sunglasses.

"Have you seen this man?" Ray showed him a picture of Johnson, which they pulled from the internet.

The security man stared at the picture for a moment. "No."

"We are looking for him, sir. Just like I explained, he is involved in a case we are investigating. He may have been with some people. Did you notice anything strange from the cars coming in and leaving through the gate?"

The man thought about it. "Wait, a black Mercedes rushed out. They failed to give me their driver's pass. Three to five people were in the car. I didn't see their faces clearly, but the driver appeared to be in haste."

Bingo, Ray thought.

"When was that?" Frank asked.

"Just now as you pulled in."

"Which road did they take?" An agent beside Frank asked.

The man pointed left. They raced back to the car. Ten seconds later, Ray drove the vehicle through the gate. He took the road by the left, and the tires screeched as he changed gear and careened the car down the road.

CHAPTER THIRTY-SIX

The lead girl stepped outside with a mobile phone, and Loretta used that opportunity to chat with the rest of the girls. The girls had given her a pair of black trousers and a red top. She was glad to remove her torn and dirty wedding gown and change to the new set of clothes.

There were ten girls in the room. Six came from the southern part of the country. The rest came from the northern region. They were excited about travelling abroad.

"We want to leave this shitty life behind," a twenty-four year old girl who sat at the edge of the table told her. Her face revealed the deep wrinkles on her temple, which made her look older than her age.

"We are leaving tomorrow," another girl said, her voice surging with anticipation.

At that moment, the door opened, and the lead girl marched in. The rest of the girls kept quiet. Loretta observed that the lead girl was furious. She held Loretta's hand and took her outside, closing the door behind them. "You lied to us," she started, her voice stern and accusatory. "You are not one of us. Who are you? An undercover cop?"

Loretta's eyes narrowed. She swallowed hard. "No."

At that moment, three men appeared at the beginning of the passageway and started approaching them. The hair at the back of Loretta's neck stood erect. She looked up and saw Raze Brown and two of his men coming close, and her newfound hope evaporated.

"Look at her," the lead girl pointed at her.

Loretta's mouth hung open as the puzzles fell into place. The lead girl had gone outside to call them as soon as she saw her. She was working with them, and the rest of the girls did not know.

"You are one of them," Loretta said to her as Raze's men took hold of her hand.

"Shut up." She heard the girl say.

Loretta turned and saw herself staring into the cold eyes of Raze Brown. An icy shiver spread through her body.

"Young woman, you have the guts to disobey my orders. I promise you, your death will be painful and slow."

Loretta's whole body began to tremble. "No, please, I'm so sorry. I won't do it again."

The lead girl shot an evil dagger at Loretta and entered through the door, closing it behind her.

Raze Brown paced the corridor, his face flushed with anger. "Call him now!"

"Yes, boss," one of his men replied.

***

Johnson's phone rang. He was driving at the pace of 80km/h along Umaru Musa Yar'Adua road. His right hand rested on the sterling while his left hand was intertwined with that of Anna. He slowed down and put the phone to his ear.

"Your time is up, tough guy. If you are not here in five minutes, I will feed her to the dog." Raze barked at the other end of the line.

Johnson calmed down his breathing even though the voice and the call irritated him. There was a reason he was called The Wise One at the cartel. He took his time to make rational decisions no matter the situation. He tried to outthink his enemies and took his time to study them before he struck.

Johnson said slowly. "Raze, the rules have changed. You don't get to say how this proceeds any longer."

"If you talk again—"

Raze was furious as usual, but Johnson no longer had time for drama. He cut in. "Check your WhatsApp for new messages." He peered at the back seat. His eyes met Luka's, and Luka signalled that it had been done. As they were talking, Luka had sent Anna's pictures to Raze on WhatsApp.

"Baby, what is going on? Who is calling you on the phone? Why are we not at the hotel yet?"

Anna's melodious voice was a distraction he didn't need right now.

"Quiet." Johnson dismissed her concerns with a wave of his hand.

Raze came on the line, barking like a wounded animal. "What is the meaning of this? You are out of your mind for pulling such a cheap trick on me."

Johnson put the phone close to Anna's face. "Say hello to Daddy."

Confusion broke across Anna's face. "Who is Daddy?" Her confusion turned into a smile. "Are you playing a game?"

"How did you...what did you do?" Raze's voice bellowed. Ray figured he had recognized the voice.

Johnson brought the phone back to his ear and relaxed on the leather seat. "I like controlling the options."

Anna was the estranged daughter of Onyeka Okpala, AKA Raze Brown. Her mum—Daniella, was once a stripper at Glorious Heights Night Club. She was one of the many women Raze slept with. But Raze cherished her more than the others. They lived together for a few years after Anna was born. But Daniella left because she couldn't tolerate the cheating and the many women he had in his life. Not wanting her partner's dangerous lifestyle to influence their daughter, Daniella left with Anna. Raze pleaded with her to stay. Daniella refused but only allowed him visiting rights when he promised to change.

Raze maintained contact with his daughter, visiting her and always bringing gifts right until she became a teenager. Until they had a scuffle after he missed her sixteenth birthday and her mother, worried about Raze's influence on their daughter, used that opportunity to put a permanent wedge between Anna and her father. She told her daughter the kind of life her father lived, and from then on, Anna wanted no part of him in her life.

Johnson had met Daniella two years ago at a friend's birthday party in Owerri. She was drawn to his powerful masculine charm and had had too much to drink that night. They met and hit it off with a one-night stand after the party, and Johnson exceeded her expectations on her bed. Daniella was in her mid-forties and had the kind of beauty that turned heads as she walked. But Johnson observed there was no wedding band on her ring finger. He was worried he was hitting on someone's wife, one of the lines he had sworn not to cross. When he asked her if she was married, her eyes welled with tears, and she looked away.

She stared into his eyes and decided that since they were both strangers and wouldn't meet again, there was no reason to hold anything back. She bared it all out and told him she wasn't married but had a daughter with a gangster named Raze Brown.

When Johnson heard the name, it hit him like cold water. It took every strength in him to stay calm and play his part as a stranger that he was. He listened as she told him her story and offered no judgement. Once she was done, he allowed her to cry on his shoulders. She didn't tell him what work she was doing at that time, and he didn't want to push his luck by prying.

After that meeting, they never met again. Still, Johnson kept the secret as insurance that would be useful in the future. Since he found out the truth about Raze's secret daughter, he'd been holding it close to his chest.

Raze kept this secret from his men while forbidding anyone to get married or have kids. He called it unnecessary baggage that would leave them weak and vulnerable to their enemies. This was why Johnson hated double standards and had broken away to follow his own path.

Johnson had always felt that Raze resisted change even when the rest of the world was changing every day. The crime lords had gone corporate. Drug trafficking and the prostitution business had become too hot. The technology used at the borders and airports could detect these illegal activities. Their men were taking many risks for a reward that had shrunk in size over the years. Worse, they did not have enough money to buy off all the corrupt immigration officials at the borders.

Johnson knew there was a smart way to do things. Having a legitimate business would give him the cover to live a normal life. It would put suspicions off his back and allow him to do whatever he desired without distractions and harassment. But Raze would never understand. That was why he broke away from the cartel and left with the men loyal to him.

Johnson hated hypocrites like Raze. His double standards reminded him of past wounds that had refused to heal. His own mother had lied to him about his father. Throughout his childhood, he believed his father had abandoned him and his mum.

Years later, when he discovered that his father was a criminal, he was angry at his mother for not telling him the truth. His mother claimed she didn't want him to end up like his father. His father was sentenced to life for murder which he committed during a botched bank robbery operation.

By the time Johnson found out the truth about his father, he had died in prison, and Johnson was already a Dragon Cartel member.

The truth he uncovered about his father made him reflect on his life. He didn't want to end up like his late father, and he started planning to come out of criminal life. He had pledged to cut off entirely from his past once he got married to Loretta. But now, his past had come back to haunt him. Well, now, he had a chance to do something about it.

"Let's make a trade. Anna for Loretta," he said to Raze on the phone.

Raze stayed silent for a few seconds. "Come to Crocodile Axis at One Man Village. You know the spot. 4 pm. If you come with law enforcement agents, you will never lay your eyes on Loretta again."

Johnson mulled a plan on his mind. It was better to be there an hour earlier and stake out the location. "Alright, I'll be there."

CHAPTER THIRTY-SEVEN

Johnson and his men, along with Anna, reached One Man Village by three in the afternoon. One Man Village was a town that lay along Keffi - Abuja expressway. It was a fast-developing town with over one million residents. The growth and expansion of Abuja had over the decades spiralled into nearby border towns and villages.

Population and urban development in towns like Mararaba, Masaka, Ado, New Karo, New Nyanya and One Man Village had skyrocketed to astonishing levels. As people moved from the capital city to these small towns, new economic activities fuelled development into these previously sparsely populated enclaves.

They drove past one-storey houses and small grocery stores until the houses disappeared and the landscape around them transformed into a stretch of bare land untouched by any form of development. He took a left and soon reached a large expanse of land surrounded by a forest at its right and a river at its left.

This place was called the Crocodile Axis. The river in the axis was rumoured to harbour crocodiles and dangerous reptiles. Residents stayed away from the Crocodile Axis. This made it the perfect spot for the members of the Dragon Cartel. This was where they usually met and planned most of their operations.

It had no houses, no sign of human life, no law enforcement presence. It was not different from a village in remote parts of the country. Johnson parked his car beside the forest, and his men spilled out with their automatic weapons and began to scout the place. When the time approached, they would take positions at strategic locations and wait for the right time to strike the enemy.

Johnson stayed behind in the car and turned to check on Anna. She glanced at him. Her eyes shone with a thousand questions, her face revealing her disappointment. He noticed she looked frightened.

"Who are you?" she managed to let out.

Johnson brought out his gun. She saw it and cringed. He wouldn't allow any harm to come to her. He just wanted Loretta back, and once she was released to him, he would let her go to her father. He hoped the exchange would go as planned. But he knew Raze was not a reasonable man. He hated doing this, but he had no option—not when dealing with an enemy who was playing by a different set of rules.

"Listen to me," he said to Anna. "I won't hurt you. I will make sure no harm comes to you. I just want you to comply. Within the next few minutes, all of this would be over."

Fear was in her eyes. She nodded, and Johnson brought out a rope and tied her hands. "Remember the rules. Don't do anything stupid. This will be over before you know it."

She gave him a curt nod. He climbed out of the car and rested his body against the vehicle, his mind deep in thought. Johnson knew his weakness were those close to him. Raze knew this and had used it hurt him today. He knew Raze wanted him and his bride dead. But when he escaped, Raze kidnapped Loretta. Johnson knew it was a ploy meant to compel him to come and rescue her so Raze could finally get his revenge by killing them both.

He, of course, had decided to level the playing field by going after his secret daughter. Raze was unpredictable, and no one knew what he would do when his temper flared. He knew how close Johnson was to his mother. Back when Johnson was his right-hand man at the cartel, Raze used to make light jokes about how Johnson was still attached to his mother's breasts. They would laugh over it while gulping down bottles of beer.

Johnson lit a cigarette and put it between his lips. He inhaled slowly and blew out the puff of smoke. The cigarette slipped from his fingers and dropped to the ground. He used his feet to crush its remaining light. His anger had rushed to the surface. He was angry at himself for making foolish mistakes that had left him vulnerable. He shouldn't have told them about his mother. He should have cut off from her long ago to keep her safe. He didn't want to rack his brain predicting every action a crazy Raze Brown would take, but he didn't want to take chances either.

He brought his mobile phone close to his ear. His mother picked up on the first ring.

"Mama, where are you?"

"Johnson, you've scared me." His mother's voice was frantic and full of motherly concern. "Where are you? Where is your bride? Today is your wedding day, for god's sake. Have you seen what they are saying in the news? Please, tell me, what is going on?"

"Mama, please, listen to me carefully."

***

Caroline Omata stood like an Iroko tree in her well-furnished room in Bolingo hotel. Her face was full of concern. A tiny tear appeared at the corner of her eyes. She refused to wipe it. It loosened its grip on her cheek and fell. She looked uncomfortable and had aged ten years within a short period.

Caroline had been standing for a while. She went back to the bed and collapsed her weight on the big mattress. She checked her phone to know if she received new messages or a missed call. Nothing. What happened at the wedding had deeply unsettled her.

When the bad news about a deadly shooting and kidnapping started floating around in the church premises, she was at a loss on what to tell her invited guests. She went to a corner of the church and cried silently, her tears leaving a crack on her face covered with mascara.

A DSS agent interviewed her, asking too many questions and making accusations. She left afterwards and took a cab to the hotel without leaving a word for anyone. She couldn't bear the shame and pity that would be in their eyes. When they find out the wedding would no longer hold, they would go back to their homes. She had a bigger problem on her hands.

Since she arrived at the hotel three hours ago, her heart had not been at ease. Her maternal instinct told her Johnson's life was in danger. She had always had suspicions that her son had a lot of enemies.

Many people were poor and hungry in this country. Becoming wealthy was like putting a mark on your back. They would kidnap your loved ones and demand ransom. It's no wonder kidnapping cases had risen in the country. The kidnappers now bargain for ransom with their victims' families and would often agree to collect ransom as low as five thousand naira. Her mind told her this was what was happening here.

Her fear was confirmed when she watched a news report where DSS stated that Loretta had been kidnapped. No one knew what happened to her son. Even the DSS agent who interviewed her when she was at the House on the Rock church could not tell her anything. Had they killed him? Or were they forcing him to pay for ransom for Loretta's release? Who would she ask? Her son's phone number was switched off. Her heart was ripping apart.

Suddenly, her phone rang. She picked it up in a hurry,

"Mama, where are you?"

Her heart leapt. She sat bolt upright on the bed. Johnson. Her son. He was alive. She placed her free hand on her chest, took a deep breath and breathed out hot air a second later, releasing her pent-up frustration. "Johnson, you've scared me. Where are you? Where is your bride? I've been worried to death. Today is your wedding day, for god's sake. Look at what they are saying in the news. Please, tell me, what is going on?"

"Mama, please, listen carefully." Caroline frowned. Her son's voice had become strange. She couldn't recognize this voice. It was bare of human emotions. This was not her Johnson. But her mind told her that this was her son. What had they done to him? "I want you to leave the city immediately."

She froze. "Why? What is going on? You have not told me anything yet." Her fears and frustration had resurfaced.

"Mama, please, do what I'm telling you. The lives of the people close to me are in danger. They took Loretta, and I don't know what they will do next. I just want to keep you safe." He paused for a long moment and continued, "Listen, some people are after my life. One of them is a mad man. They are envious of my success. They want to destroy my life and take everything that belongs to me."

Tears filled Caroline's eyes. "I knew it," she said with conviction. This had confirmed her worst fears. "Where should I go?

"Good, take a flight back to Lagos. Go to the Airport now. Once you reach Lagos, take a cab to Abeokuta. Do you remember the house I told you I was building at Abeokuta?"

"The one at No 3 Obada road."

"Yes, I have completed and furnished the building. Once you reach there, collect the keys from the gateman. He knows who you are."

"Yes, we met when you and I visited the construction site when the building was at its roofing stage."

"No one else knows of its existence. Go to the Airport now. I will call you back later."

"Johnson..." She heard the click. He had hung up. She rushed and began to zip up her bag. Once she was done, she rose and headed to the door with the bag. She turned the doorknob but hesitated on second thought.

What was the fate of her daughter-in-law? She hadn't gotten any meaningful update about her son and his bride from watching the news since she got here. Instead, fake news alleged that her son was a member of a criminal cartel. She knew this was not true. She would sue those peddlers of false information once this madness was over.

She went back and sank on her bed. She couldn't just run away and hide. Johnson needed her help. She heard it in his voice. He had helped to erase their suffering. Now, it was her turn to help him. She hoped this would help clear his name as well. She picked up the card on the stool beside her bed. She stared at the card for a long time. She made the decision and dialled the number.

CHAPTER THIRTY-EIGHT

Ray drove for ten minutes but didn't see any black Mercedes. He slowed down and finally eased the car beside the door and sighed.

"This shows that Johnson was here," one of the agents at the backseat said.

"We are not certain, but it appears so," Ray said.

"They have gotten away," Frank observed.

Ray wound down the window and peered out. "Yes, and we don't know where they are. If he is alive and is the one that just came to this University, it begs the question; what is he doing here? How is he connected to all of this? Is he knowingly putting his bride's life in danger?"

"Did he order the hit himself so he could disappear?" the second agent at the back said.

"I heard Breya when he said we should find Raze Brown," Frank chipped in.

"We still don't know who he is or where he is. What we know is that he is connected to this case," said Ray.

"He may be one of the leaders of the cartel," Frank said.

Ray nodded. His eyes narrowed as an idea entered his mind. "Johnson is the key to this investigation. If we find him, we will find Loretta and the people holding her hostage. And we will solve this case."

As Frank nodded in agreement, his phone rang, and he put it on speaker.

"Am I speaking to Agent Frank?"

"It's Caroline Omata," Frank whispered. Silence fell inside the car.

"Yes, madam, this is DSS Agent Frank Igwe."

"What I told you is the truth. My son's and his bride's lives are in danger. Some group of people are after his life. They want to take everything away from him."

Frank frowned. "Alright, calm down, ma'am. You said this earlier today. How did you know this?"

"He called me." Her voice showed she was frustrated at not being understood.

Everyone in the car became alert as they paid attention.

"Who called you?"

"My son, Johnson."

Frank brought out a notepad. "When was that?"

"A few minutes ago. Please, investigate this and catch these criminals who attacked them today. My son is a law-abiding citizen who pays his taxes. He has provided funds to many youths, which enabled them to start their businesses. Is this how greedy and heartless people want to pay him back? Now, what will his country do about this? Please, I want your agency to stop them. Catch them. Don't let them get away."

"Ma'am, thank you very much for your cooperation. We will not let any harm come to your son or his bride. We will rescue them. One last question; did he tell you where he is?"

"No." The line disconnected.

Ray had already dialled a number. "Christine, I want you to run a trace on this number."

Ray and his former colleague, Christine Zainab, had worked together when he was a DSS analyst. She was still one of the top analysts in their branch office. When Ray became HATU team leader, he wasted no time getting permission to reassign her to his team and on this case.

"Go on."

Ray stared at Frank's call log and called out Caroline Omata's digits to her hearing. "I want you to run a trace on the number that called her less than ten minutes ago and get us a location."

"I'm on it, sir."

***

Raze, and his men were set to leave for One Man Village. Three Sedan vehicles sat on the red sand of the open field. The sun was harsh and blazing hot. The sun rays shining on the car windows refracted on their faces. The place was eerie quiet except for sounds from his men who were putting magazines into their weapons.

Loretta sat in the first vehicle. Her hands were tied. A black cloth was pulled over her head.

Raze was surrounded by ten of his men, all outfitted with automatic weapons. The rest of the men would stay behind on the farm. Two of his men were snipers. He had given them explicit orders on what he needed them to do.

Duru, who had done his job well and had gotten back on Raze's good graces, approached him. "Boss, do you have to join us? Let me and the rest of the men go. Once he arrives, we will take Anna, and our men will do their job. We will bring back your daughter safely."

Raze was still furious that Johnson had the gut to go after his beloved daughter. Johnson had taken a step too far. He was glad that today would be Johnson's last day on earth. He and his bride.

He fixed his gaze at his revolver, and after oiling it, he began to assemble the gun.

"I will do this myself. Once we make the exchange and Anna is back at my side, we will surround him and his men. Oh, I know he will come with his men. That arrogant boy. He will watch me pull the trigger that will end his bride's life," he said through gritted teeth, "then,

I will look into his eyes and empty the rest of the bullets into his skull and put an end to his miserable life."

He finished assembling his revolver and turned to face his men. "Let's go. If anything goes wrong, you know what to do. They must never leave that place alive."

"Yes, sir," the muscled men replied in unison.

They entered the three cars and launched into the hot Saturday weather.

CHAPTER THIRTY-NINE

Crocodile Axis, One Man Village

After speaking with his mother, Johnson gave orders to his men, and they took their position. He made a call, and the rest of his men, who were five in number, arrived thirty minutes later in a pickup truck. Their heavy boots hit the ground as they stepped out of the car. They carried AK-47 rifles and shook hands with the rest of the team.

As four in the evening approached, the men took position inside the forest. No one would know they were there. Johnson had already told them to look for the snipers and take them out with silenced weapons. He knew how Raze operated. There was no other hidden place to stay apart from the forest. Only Anna and three of his men, Luka, Caleb, and Ugo, stayed with him as they waited for Raze and his men.

All the men carried auto rifles. Johnson had untied the rope at Anna's wrists. He whispered in her ears. She nodded, but fear seemed to have lodged permanently at the corner of her eyes.

Raze, and his men arrived five minutes to four. They came in three black Sedan vehicles. Johnson watched as Raze opened his side of the passenger door and stepped out of the car. He wore an earbud just like the rest of his men and carried a revolver.

He opened the door beside the driver's seat, and a woman whose hands were tied stepped out. He pulled out a black cloth that covered her head, and Johnson felt tightness in his chest. *Loretta*. His bride. At that moment, his eyes met with Raze's and the lunatic smirked at him.

Raze untied Loretta's hands and held her by the hand as the team walked briefly and stopped beside the river. Johnson didn't see the snipers. They might have stepped out of one of the vehicles somewhere along the route to this axis. He watched as Raze said something to his men, and they turned and faced Johnson and his men. At that instant, Anna saw her dad and made to run, but Luka raised his gun. "Don't. Not yet time."

***

Loretta's heart was racing. She had already heard Raze talking to his men. If they had allowed her to listen to what she was not supposed to hear, it meant she wouldn't leave this place alive. And Johnson too. Whatever Johnson did to Raze, it was clear to her that he wanted to carry out his own revenge today—in this middle of nowhere. How could she warn Johnson that all of this was a trap?

She was still in deep thought when a hand touched her on the shoulders. She looked up. It was the monster. "Young lady, your fiancé has come to rescue you. You are free to go." He flashed her a broad smile, and for the first time, she saw his tobacco-stained teeth.

She tried to run, but her legs refused.

Someone tapped her shoulder with the muzzle of a gun. "Go!"

She turned and saw Johnson and his men holding their weapons. They were waiting for her. As she looked at him and his men, he looked like a stranger. It was as though what Raze said about him was true. Did she really know anything about him? She saw a young girl rushing towards Raze and his men. Anna. She'd heard she was Raze's daughter. She banished the doubts and welcomed a glimmer of hope that flashed through her mind. They might survive this. She ran as far as her weak legs could carry her—towards Johnson and his men, to her freedom.

***

"Father!" Anna screamed as she ran to meet Raze. Tears fell from her eyes and rolled down her cheeks. Raze approached her and enveloped her in a warm embrace. "It's alright, Anna. I'm so sorry you had to go through this. Everything is alright now." He led her towards a narrow path beside the river and spoke to his men through the throat microphone. "Kill his men and bring me the couple. Now!"

Suddenly, the sound of a bullet pierced through the quiet atmosphere, and the shooting started.

CHAPTER FORTY

Everything moved fast. Within seconds, the Crocodile Axis had turned into a warzone as men from the opposing forces engaged each other in a fiery gun battle.

When Raze gave the order, he thought his men would easily mow down the three men Johnson came with. But his eyes widened when more men poured out of the forest and joined Johnson. He watched as men from both sides began to fall. No, this wasn't the plan. He spoke into his mic. "Charlie, go ahead and take out the couple now." But he heard no voice. Stunned, he said again, "Jamba, are you there?" Silence. He tried to raise the snipers but couldn't. The reality hit him hard on the face. This bastard and his men had killed them. Did he underestimate them? No, this ends today, he assured himself.

He looked beside him and saw Duru. "Duru, what are you waiting for?"

"Sir."

"Go after them. This battle should have ended five minutes ago."

Duru moved away from his side and ran to support his colleagues. The moment Duru left, Raze stared ahead and saw Johnson distracted by Loretta. He was shielding her close to a tree while dodging bullets and firing back. He took his chance. He took aim and pulled the trigger.

***

Johnson was whispering in Loretta's ear when he grunted in pain. Loretta's eyes widened as she watched him grasp his bleeding shoulder with one of his hands.

He looked ahead and saw Raze holding Anna and escaping through the narrow path beside the river. "No." He had Loretta, and they both chased Raze through the tight route.

Duru saw them and made to pull the trigger, but a bullet from Johnson's gun blew away his forehead. Johnson considered it a perfect payback for his betrayal. He didn't want to let his guard down again. Another gunman tried to raise his gun, but Johnson launched his knife, which caught him squarely in the stomach. They entered the tiny road, and Johnson sighted Raze dragging Anna against her wish.

"Let me go," Anna was saying.

"No, they will kill you."

Johnson raised his gun and fired. The bullet caught Raze in his stomach.

"Aaah." Raze moaned and fired back, but Johnson and Loretta ducked in time and dodged it. Anna continued to scream but Raze held her tight and kept shooting blindly at their direction.

"Freeze. Drop your weapon now. This is DSS," a voice ordered from a blaring microphone.

Johnson froze. He wondered how they knew. When he and Loretta turned and peeped at the other road, they saw many DSS agents exiting four different vehicles. The DSS men quickly surrounded most of the men except those who were firing from the forest.

Johnson stared at Raze and saw him running away with his daughter. He had already given them a huge gap. Johnson looked back at his men. The DSS agents were approaching, and soon they would see him and arrest him. He squeezed his eyes shut and made a quick decision. "Honey, run to DSS agents. You will be safe there."

Loretta stared at his bleeding shoulder. "No, what about you? You are bleeding. Surrender to them. I'm sure they will get you the treatment you need. I'll testify on your behalf and tell them the truth about what happened today. I know you lied to me, but you don't deserve to die."

Johnson shook his head. "You won't understand." He fixed his gaze at her. "Don't worry, I'll be fine. I'm sorry about everything. I will explain everything to you later. Now, run."

Loretta ran, and as she did, her eyes met with Ray's where he was amid several DSS agents, and she was stunned and continued to stare at him in disbelief. At that moment, different memories flashed through her mind all at once. She slowed down her pace, and in that instant, a bullet hit her, and she screamed and fell.

CHAPTER FORTY-ONE

Ray watched as Loretta ran towards him and his team. He observed as she slowed her pace. He didn't know why, and then out of nowhere, a bullet hit her, and she fell. His heart clenched, and he, along with Frank and four agents, ran to where she fell. He bent down and stared into her eyes. She was alive, but her pulse was weak. They were losing her.

Christine had come through and given them a location where Johnson's call came from. A place called Crocodile Axis in One Man Village along Abuja – Keffi Highway. Thanks to GPS and satellite technology, he and a team he assembled with his boss' permission were able to locate this place. This team was part of 'Operation Slay the Dragon' that they had launched at their Abuja Central Branch an hour ago. He had hoped they were not too late, but now, it was as though they were.

"Get a medic here. We need to rush her to the hospital," Ray shouted.

Two people carried Loretta and started heading to one of the cars. Ray followed them. "Stay with me Loretta, you will be fine."

She slit her eyes open, and their gaze met. "They are holding some girls on a farm. You need to rescue them." Her voice was weak.

"Please come again," Ray said. "Which girls? Where?"

Silence. He stared at her and discovered that her eyes had closed. She had slipped into unconsciousness.

Ray issued series of orders to his men. Frank interrupted him as he was speaking. "Ray, we have started arresting the gunmen, but Johnson and Raze are not here."

Frank's words hit him hard. He stared at the faces of the men they had arrested. Two DSS agents were dragging three wounded criminals out of the forest. But the big guns were not there. At that instant, he heard a wild scream. He listened again. "Let me go!" It was the voice of a girl.

Ray left his men and ran cautiously towards the small path where the scream was coming from. The girl's shrill voice got louder as he entered the tiny road and started running as far as he could go. He didn't see Johnson. Where was he? He should have asked Loretta, but she was unconscious.

The road was carved out of the forest. Ray raced warily. The road was filled with weeds. The forest was beginning to claim it back, probably because the villagers had stopped using it. He knew that narrow paths like this could be dangerous. They were always filled with snakes and dangerous reptiles.

"Let me go." The voice got louder. He reached a place where the road transformed into three different routes. He entered the road by the left and saw a wounded man he guessed was in his late forties dragging a young girl in her early twenties while she struggled to escape from his grip. Ray crept closer towards him. He figured this was Raze Brown. Blood covered the hands he placed on his stomach.

"Freeze. This is DSS. Drop your weapon. Don't move an inch."

Suddenly, Raze turned to face him. He held the girl by the neck and placed his gun on her head. His quick movement happened within seconds. The girl's eyes were filled with terror. "No agent. Drop your weapon, or I will shoot her, and her blood will be in your hands."

Ray watched him in stunned silence, his brain perusing through many options on how to come out of this and still save the young girl's life, but he came up empty.

"Father, what are you doing? Let me go."

"Keep quiet, Anna."

Ray's eyes widened as his mind made the connection. The two letters 'AN' written in the card he and Frank saw in Johnson's apartment were Anna's abbreviation. This meant Anna was a student at the University of Abuja. Raze took Johnson's bride, and Johnson went to the university campus and took Anna. But how was Johnson able to pull it off? Did he kidnap Anna, or she knew who he was?

Wait a minute. If Anna called Raze 'father', it meant she was Raze Brown's daughter.

Oh my God. Ray stared at Raze. The man was crazy. "You want to kill your daughter to save your own life. Isn't that what is going on here?"

Raze shot three bullets into the air, and Anna screamed. "I'll do it. Drop your weapon now."

Ray discovered he had been put in a tight spot. This man was crazy, no doubt. Ray wouldn't put the young girl's life at risk.

As he bent to put his gun on the ground, Anna let out a shrill cry and twisted herself fiercely from Raze's grip. Her sudden action made Raze lose his bearing for a second. He tried to catch her, and three successive bullets hit him squarely on the chest. He cried out in shock, and his limp body collapsed on the red earth.

CHAPTER FORTY-TWO

Ray was astonished as he watched the scene unfold. He looked beside him and saw Frank step forward. He still had the gun in his hands. Ray stared at his partner, whose eyes shone with curiosity.

"I heard her scream. I followed you. When I saw how crazy he was to want to kill his own daughter, I knew I had to take the shot," Frank said and extended his right hand. Ray took it, and Frank dragged him up.

"Thanks, mate," Ray said. They ran and met Anna, where she lay at the ground whimpering beside her father's corpse.

Ray bent down beside her. "Hi Anna, my name is Ray Okon. I am a DSS agent with Homicide and Anti-Drug Trafficking Unit. You are safe now. He can't harm you anymore."

Anna nodded and sobbed silently. They helped her to stand, and the trio went back and joined the rest of the team.

"Where is Loretta?" Ray asked as soon as he reunited with his men.

"Our medic van, the only one we came with, took her to Central District Medical Centre. They are on their way now," An agent beside Ray responded.

Ray released a sigh of relief. They handcuffed the rest of the men. Out of twenty men, ten were killed in the gunfire, and nine were arrested. Raze Brown was dead, but no one had seen Johnson Omata—the only one who was missing.

"We have done great work here. Let's go," Frank said.

"No," Ray said. He approached one of the handcuffed criminals. "Where are the girls? Where are you keeping them?"

The handcuffed man stared at him in puzzlement.

"Which girls? I no know wetin you dey talk about," he said in Pidgin English.

"You are keeping them inside a farm. Where is it?" Ray shouted. He was losing his patience. He ordered his men to interrogate the criminals and break their legs if they must. They were not leaving there without that information.

Three DSS agents interrogated the gangsters. One of them talked when an agent put the muzzle of his gun inside his mouth and threatened to pull the trigger. He told them the location of the farm even as his mates signalled him with their eyes to keep quiet.

Ray and his men took the arrested men back to their DSS branch, where they would get them ready to be charged to court. They also took Anna with them, and she was lodged in a hotel close to their office. Two agents were assigned to her room.

Ray briefed his boss about the new development in the case, and he was assigned a 30-man team that he would use for the remaining operation.

By six in the evening, the team arrived at the large farm in Kilome. When they reached the worn-out iron gate, gunfire erupted. The bullets blasted at their vehicles, killing five agents on the spot as they stepped out of their cars.

The gunfire came from men stationed outside the gate. But a thirty-man DSS team was too much for the drug dealers to handle. The agents returned fire, and a gun battle started. The officers surrounded the building and engaged the criminals until their bullets ran out. Ten criminals died in the violent shootout, and five were arrested.

Ray and his team secured the farm and rescued the girls. One of the girls who appeared to be their leader pulled out a handgun, but an agent standing at her back tackled her before she could pull the trigger. Ray observed that most of the girls were confused at what they saw. They didn't know what they had gotten themselves into. It was a deception on a large scale.

They searched through the five buildings in the sixty hectares of land and rescued girls in worse conditions. They were in a dark basement. They were too skinny, their eyes hollow and their hands bound together with a long rope. They recovered huge stacks of naira notes and bags of cocaine, heroin, and tramadol. For the next three days, DSS agents worked with the police to arrest more criminals who were members of the cartel and street dealers who helped them push the drugs into the city.

***

The DSS branch office in Abuja central district was surrounded by newsmen and their camera crews. It was Wednesday afternoon, and the temperature was not yet ready to slow down its climb. Weather experts had predicted that today would be the hottest day in July. DSS senior officer, Ezekiel Bassey, stepped out of the front door with agents Ray and Frank and faced the newsmen. For the past three days, news of the arrest of the Dragon Cartel members had taken the media by surprise. They had been calling, demanding information.

That morning, Ezekiel had a meeting with his agents after speaking with his bosses at the headquarters. They agreed to schedule a press briefing at noon. Only invited newsmen and journalists would be allowed to join in the briefing.

Ezekiel reached a podium covered with an array of microphones bearing different news agencies and media outlets' labels. Camera lights flashed at his face. He smiled at the small crowd.

"Thank you all for coming. We've been tracking a set of criminals for the past three years. These men who are members of the Dragon Cartel have been hurting our city, pumping all kinds of illicit drugs into the streets. This year, they turned to murder and violent criminal activities as they grew confident and arrogant in their crimes." He paused, wiped his face with a white handkerchief and continued. "We also got reports that they operate prostitution rings. They lure our young women into their traps, promising them a better life in Italy and Dubai. Their victims are sent to these countries and forced into prostitution. Those who find out the truth and try to escape are killed in cold blood."

"To stop these criminals and put them behind bars, we launched operation Slay the Dragon," he paused and looked at Ray, who stood by his side. "I'm glad to announce that last Saturday, my men followed a credible Intel after an attack on a couple who were on their way to their wedding. The Intel led them to the lair of these criminals. Since Saturday, my men have been busy with the investigation. We've arrested their members. Those who resisted were killed. We lost some of our men in the process. They died while keeping our city safe, and for that, they are our heroes. However, we have dismantled their criminal organisation and their prostitution rings. We've recovered illicit drugs worth millions of Naira. I'm glad to announce to you that our capital city is safe and our young men and girls are safe as well. We can take your questions."

A flurry of questions started the moment he stopped speaking.

"Sir, what about the leader of the cartel? He was not mentioned in the reports released to the media by your agency."

"He resisted arrest and was shot dead before he could claim more innocent lives," Ezekiel replied and pointed to a female NTA journalist. "Next, yes, Rachel."

"Sir, we got reports that DSS has not yet caught one of the masterminds, Johnson Omata. Please, what can you tell us about this?"

"He escaped during the attack. Johnson has deceived the public for so long. His days are numbered. Right now, he is the most wanted criminal in Nigeria. I have activated a nationwide manhunt for him. We will catch him, and he will face the full wrath of the law."

"Sir, what is the fate of the arrested men? Where are they right now?" one of the journalists in the crowd asked.

"Our lawyers have started criminal proceedings against them. They will soon be arraigned in court."

An AIT journalist raised her hand. "Sir, there are rumours that the criminals had an insider in your agency who worked with them and supplied them with valuable information. If this is true, where is this insider? Has he been arrested? Will he be prosecuted?"

Sadness broke across Ezekiel's face. He looked straight into the cameras. "The rumours are true. It's a sad page in this case that we want to close as quickly as possible. He has been arrested and is in our custody. Of course, he will be prosecuted with the rest of the criminals. The informant was one of our agents, a rotten egg. As I said, we have started criminal proceedings against them."

More questions flew in. Ezekiel wiped the sweat off his temple and said, "That will be all. Thank you." He stepped out of the podium and entered the building with his agents.

***

After the press briefing, Ray headed straight to his car and drove to the Central District Medical Centre. It was just fifteen minutes away from their branch office. He had already taken permission from his boss. This was something he needed to do. He was glad they had made progress on the case.

A day earlier, his boss had allowed Anna to be discharged after briefing them and giving a statement. She'd pleaded she didn't want to go back to school. Instead, she wanted to go back to Owerri, where she lived with her mother. Ezekiel Bassey assigned an agent to travel with her. The agent reported seven hours later that she had reached home safely.

Ray reached the hospital and made his way to Loretta's ward. There was no drip or IV tube on her hand. Her stomach was covered with a bandage. His face brightened when he discovered she was awake. Two days ago, when he came here, she was still unconscious. He had stayed vigil by her side throughout the night.

According to the doctor he'd met on Monday morning, the bullet grazed through her right abdomen and made a clean exit. However, it caused her internal bleeding. The doctor and his team had to work for hours to stop the bleeding.

"She is getting treatment. She is a fighter. She will be fine," Dr Andrew had told him.

Now, as he stared into Loretta's eyes, watching her smile, a surge of happiness swept through him.

"Hi," her voice was soft, like a symphony.

"Hi," Ray replied.

They stared at each other for a long moment enjoying the silence. Ray didn't know when he began to walk down memory lane. During their university days, they would stay together in his house, watch movies during the weekend and just stay quiet for hours, enjoying each other's silence.

With Loretta, he didn't have to pretend. They were always comfortable in each other's company. A tear appeared at the corner of Ray's right eye as he remembered the distant memory of their beautiful past—of what used to be.

He met her gaze and was stunned to see her shimmering eyes. Were they thinking the same thing?

Loretta brought out her hand and entwined it in his, her grip weak. "Thank you for saving my life. If you and your men didn't come when you did, I would have been dead by now."

Ray shook his head. He didn't want her to stress herself by talking too much. "No, you don't have to—"

"I insist," she said.

He smiled. He knew her more than anyone else.

She was strong and determined—a trait that enabled her to succeed both in school and in her business, despite the crippling challenges she faced.

"Those men are heartless," she said. "Especially their leader, Raze Brown." Curiosity flashed across her face. "What happened to him?"

"We stopped him before he could kill his own daughter."

Loretta became silent as surprise registered on her face.

Ray leaned closer to her. "Loretta, you are stronger than you think. You are so brave for going through such pain on a day supposed to be your wedding day. Thank you for telling us about the girls. We have rescued them. Because of you, they are safe."

A full smiled appeared on her face.

The door opened, and Cynthia came in. She saw Loretta and rushed to her bed. "Oh, Loretta, I'm so sorry, baby girl. You have gone through so much," Cynthia said and broke into a silent sob.

Tears dropped from Loretta's eyes down her cheeks. It was difficult for Ray to watch. The pain he felt for her hit him like a physical blow, sending a sharp spasm through his chest.

Two minutes later, Cynthia wiped her tears and glanced at Ray. "Ray, thank you so much for what you have done for her."

The doctor entered the moment Ray opened his mouth to respond. He rose and greeted Dr Andrew. The doctor examined Loretta and asked her a series of questions. She replied, and he scribbled on his notepad. When he was through, he turned to face Ray.

"Doctor, when will she be ready to go back home?" Ray asked.

"I'm glad she is making a fast recovery. She will be discharged after four days. I have already told her not to do exercise or engage in any stressful activity for one month. We don't want anything that will rip the wounds apart."

"What about the other women?"

"One died when she was brought here. Others are still in critical condition. They are receiving treatment. I'm afraid that some of them may suffer trauma due to what they passed through. It appeared they stayed in the dark basement for months and sometimes without food."

Ray clenched his jaw as fury crawled up his spine. These criminals had no conscience. He wished they were already behind bars. He hoped they would be given severe punishment in court for their atrocities.

He thanked Dr Andrew, greeted Loretta and Cynthia, and left the hospital. He drove back to his office. There was one last puzzle to fix—one last business to deal with in this case, and his heart would finally be at peace. Johnson Omata.

CHAPTER FORTY-THREE

Abeokuta
Three days later

The man in the vast living room was in a hurry.

Every few seconds, he would stare at the big clock on the wall and curse under his breath. He was not as fast as he wanted to be. He opened his small Echolac bag, folded five T-shirts and three pairs of trousers and put them in the bag. He winced in pain when he tried to move.

Once he'd escaped from the Crocodile Axis, he'd taken series of buses that brought him to Ibadan while he reeled under intense pain. From there, he'd taken a short bus ride to Abeokuta. At the city of Abeokuta, he'd taken a cab that dropped him off at his house in 3 Obada Road. This meant he was on the road for forty-eight hours, spending the nights in shitty hotels.

Once he'd reached his house, he'd met with his mother, who had been staying there just like he'd told her, and they arranged for a doctor she knew to come and treat his bullet wound. The doctor came in from Shagamu, removed the bullet that lodged for two days in his shoulder and cleaned up the injury. It was the ten worst minutes of his life, but he was glad he was still alive.

His mother didn't ask him questions or lay accusations when they met. The truth was out of the bag. What would she have done? She abandoned him when she could no longer take care of them both, and the streets claimed him as their own. When he was finally able to stand on his feet, he had forgiven her and wiped decades-long suffering out of her face.

He still remembered the look on her face when he arrived at the house and met her gaze as she came out of the kitchen—the look of guilt. He hoped she would forgive herself and forget about the past.

"Don't you want to eat anything?" His mother called out from the kitchen. Her voice brought him back from his distant thoughts.

He frowned. "No, I'm alright."

He put on his shirt, attached his cufflinks, and wore his trousers. He was almost through. As he tried to walk, the pain of the past few days exerted its weight on him. He'd gotten a little satisfaction when he watched the news and discovered that the monster was dead. What happened over the past seven days had ruffled him.

As he browsed through the news and the internet, his heart shattered. The media and internet mob had ripped him apart. All the good he had done with his wealth had been quickly forgotten. The same crowd who praised him on Instagram when he did giveaways were now tearing him apart on Twitter. Hashtags #ArrestJohnsonOmatanow and #Whereisthedrugdealer were trending on Social Media. They had thrown him under the bus.

He didn't even know where Loretta was or if she was still alive. Raze, and his men were determined to kill them both. He knew. It pained him that he couldn't protect them both and had to save his own skin when she needed him the most. The look of shock in her eyes when she finally saw him for who he was would forever be etched in his memory.

But if he had seen her again, would he be able to face her? What exactly would he say? Where would he begin to explain?

Their relationship was built on lies, and he was sorry for lying to her. That was too late now.

He locked the thought away and focused on finishing his packing. He needed to get going. He was running out of time.

He put a Gucci wristwatch inside and closed the bag. He heard a slight noise, and his hand went for the heckler and Koch by his side.

"Don't move. Put your hands where I can see them. It's over, Johnson."

Johnson's face lost colour. He put his hands on his head and turned. He saw an athletic DSS agent who led uniformed men into his house. He'd seen this agent before. Was that in Crocodile Axis? Wasn't he the one who led the men that raided the place and made the arrests?

His chest tightened, and his strength faded. How did they know about this place? He took all precautions. How did they get in without him knowing? Oh, he'd left the front door open because he was rushing to get to the border.

His plan had been to slightly change his appearance if the immigration agents were also looking for him and travel to the Nigerian border. He would then use bribes to cross over to Ghana. Next, he would take a flight to Dubai with his Ghanaian passport. From there, he would head straight to Qatar and stay hidden within the bowels of the Middle East, where nobody would ever find him. He'd perfected the plan for days. Now, he'd run out of options. But how did they find out he was here?

***

Ray observed when he got into the house with his men that Johnson was ready to escape. Two days ago, Ray had requested a record of the phone calls between Johnson and his mother. Christine had retrieved them while tracing Johnson's location last Saturday.

On Thursday, Ray tried to put himself in Johnson's shoes.

Johnson had run out of options. If Johnson escaped Abuja, he would seek refuge in his house at Abeokuta, which he'd mentioned to his mother. He'd promised his mother that they would meet again.

It was a big gamble for Ray, but he was used to taking risks.

The next thing Ray did was to contact the Abeokuta DSS branch and have them send a surveillance team to Johnson's house at Obada road. The three-man squad spotted a woman and a younger man talking in the living room that evening. They reported to Ray, and he travelled to Abeokuta the next day.

The Abeokuta branch assigned him a team of six agents who would aid him in the operation, and this morning, they struck.

If they had waited a moment longer, they would never have captured Johnson. There was no need to waste any more time. Ray and his men surrounded Johnson, and one of the officers handcuffed the criminal.

All of a sudden, a tall, huge woman who wore an apron strode into the living room, seething with anger. "Leave him alone. Enough of all the harassment."

Ray's politeness had reached its limit. He glanced at the roaring lioness. "Woman, keep quiet, or you will be arrested as an accomplice to your son's crimes. The list is long if you want to know."

Caroline Omata stayed by the corner, her figure subdued. She watched as one of the agents read Johnson his rights.

As they led Johnson out of the house, he turned to Ray. "I just want to ask one question."

"Go ahead."

"What about Loretta? Is she still alive and safe?"

Ray clenched his jaw. Hadn't he done enough damage to her and her reputation? He didn't want to say it out loud. "Yes, she is."

The following two days—Sunday and Monday, were tight and hectic for Ray and the agency.

On Friday, a female judge in Abuja High Court found Breya guilty of aiding and abetting criminals and obstructing an investigation launched to stop them. He was also found guilty of being an accomplice to murder and giving the Dragon Cartel members classified information about witnesses.

She found Johnson and the rest of the criminals guilty of murder, dealing in illicit drugs, human trafficking, and operating prostitution rings. For cooperating with the DSS, Breya was sentenced to seven years in prison. The judge sentenced the rest of the criminals to life in prison, and guards loaded them off to Abuja Penitentiary.

***

The next Monday, Ray was back to work. It was the first week of August, and the sky was bright.

He had attained hero status at the agency. Reports credited him for being the agent who led his team to catch the criminals hurting the city and dismantle their criminal networks. He waved at his colleagues as he headed straight to his office.

Frank entered his office a minute later, and they chatted for ten minutes before Ray's phone rang.

"Boss wants you to come to his office," Martin said as soon as he picked the call.

Ray excused himself and entered his boss' office five minutes later.

The moment Ezekiel Bassey saw him, he rose, greeted him in a firm handshake and gave him a seat. "You and your team did an impressive job, Agent Ray."

Ray knew his boss hated long talks. He thought the words were sudden. He didn't know what to say and decided to just listen.

"You remind me of myself when I was a young agent like you." Ezekiel smiled and reached for a small, framed photograph sitting on his desk. He placed it in front of Ray.

Ray saw a younger Ezekiel in his full DSS uniform. He looked energetic, and his eyes blazed with dedication and love for his country.

Ray had always known that his boss was exceptionally good at his job. He still looked agile and fit even now Ezekiel was edging closer to his sixties. A wide grin appeared on his face. "Thank you, sir, for the compliment."

"I read your file and knew right then that you will be an asset to the agency, and now, you have made us all proud."

"Thank you, sir."

Ezekiel scanned through his desk and saw what he was looking for. He brought out a file. "This is from the headquarters. You now have two important roles in the agency. You will remain as the leader of HATU, and now, you are the director of operations in the agency's Criminal Investigation Department."

Ray's eyes widened. He couldn't believe it. The famous DSS CID. It had always been his dream to be part of that elite team right from when he was still frustrated at being stuck at the desk. "Sir, I don't know what to—"

"The agency recognized your unique leadership qualities. The way you handled this investigation and organized different teams that raided the dugout of these criminals leaves no one in doubt of what you can help the agency achieve when given a higher responsibility."

Ezekiel rose and gave Ray the file containing the letter signed by the DSS director-general and shook his hands. "Continue the good work, Agent Ray. I have approved your request to take a one-month vacation. You deserve it. Rest and come back stronger."

"I'm honoured, sir. Thank you very much."

As Ray stepped out of the office, tears dropped from his eyes. They were not tears of sorrow. The tears were symbolic for him and captured how he felt right now. Now, the pain he felt for what happened to his father had eased off. The driver behind his father's death was not caught, but a feeling of fulfilment finally surged through him. He was ultimately helping to fix the broken system and put the bad guys behind bars. As he walked back to his office, he allowed himself to smile.

EPILOGUE

One Month Later

Ray lay on a mat in Jabi Park's garden, sipping pineapple juice while enjoying the cool breeze beneath the Dogonyaro trees. Dark sunglasses and a paperback novel titled The Fishermen by Chigozie Obioma sat beside him on the mat.

Ray loved coming here, sometimes after a hectic week, especially to savour the freshness nature offered. This was the last weekend of his vacation, and there was no place else he would rather be. He had just finished taking a boat ride in the lake beside the park. Now, he was relaxing under the natural air.

He watched the beautiful people who came to enjoy their lives to the fullest. It was Sunday afternoon in the last week of August. Fever by Wizkid featuring Tiwa Savage was blaring from the speaker of the local DJ.

"Mind if I join you?"

Ray heard the sweet, musical voice as it sailed on the soft breeze and caressed him. He recognized the voice and turned to where it came from. His jaw dropped when his eyes met hers. *What in the world?*

"Loretta, what are you doing here? How did you find me?" His eyes raked in her hot body.

She wore only a bikini, looking strikingly beautiful.

His breath caught in his throat.

There was a rolled-up mat in her hand. Her body was flawless, her smile easy and effortless. She didn't look like she was in a hospital a month ago.

She flashed him her gap-toothed smile. "You are keeping a lady waiting."

Oh, he had forgotten.

"I'm sorry. Please, join me." He showed her with his hand where to place her mat. She rolled it on the ground beside him and sat close to him.

He offered the fruit drink he'd brought.

She took it and sipped with a new straw he gave her. "Oh, it's delicious." Her expression brightened.

"I knew this is one of your most favourite places in the world. You love coming here during the weekend, and you are having a vacation. Perfect. It's serene, a place away from the madness in the city," she answered the question in his mind.

Ray stared at her. She knew him more than he gave her credit for. Had she been studying him lately? He still wondered how she knew he would be here by this time.

"I called Frank," she blurted, "interrogated him over the phone, and he gave you up."

They both laughed and afterwards enjoyed the silence and the quiet atmosphere for the next five minutes and watched the water in a nearby fountain rise and then got blown by the wind. For Ray, it was a beautiful sight to behold.

"I'm sorry for everything that happened," she let out.

The words caught Ray off-guard. It punched him hard like a cannonball he wasn't expecting. He turned and stared into her eyes.

She started speaking fast. "I thought I knew what I was doing. I wanted my life to be perfect. I wanted to focus on growing my business. But in the midst of it all, I took many things for granted. I forgot the only person who encouraged me to chase my dreams—the man who stood by me in my darkest days. I forgot the most important person in my life. The truth is—at a point, I didn't know what I was chasing. I guess my friend Cynthia made it worst by telling me what she thought I wanted to hear. She wanted me to come out of my shell and experiment, meet new people and have fun and—"

"No, you don't have to say all that," Ray protested.

"No, I want to. I ended up getting hooked to a killer and drug dealer who wore the cloak of an honest businessman. He sold me nothing but illusions. None of the things he told me about himself was true. But by then, I was far gone off the rail..." her voice trailed off. She paused for a moment, her face contemplative.

Ray observed she'd been doing a lot of thinking. He had too.

"Beneath the strong exterior everyone says I have," she continued, her voice fragile. "Sometimes, I am just a fearful little girl who doesn't want to end up like her mother. Now I know that sometimes, you have to pass through a dark tunnel to appreciate the light." She held her hand in his. "Ray, you are the light in my life. We've come a long way. We have always been there for each other. It's still hard for me to believe I once let you go. I'm sorry for everything that happened between us."

Ray was overwhelmed by a barrage of emotions that coursed through him. She bared herself to him. It must have taken a lot of courage for her to do that. At that moment, a silent sob tore out of her throat, and she broke down in tears. Ray didn't know when tears filled his eyes nor when he leaned forward, held her wet face in his hands and covered her mouth with his lips. Their kiss became needy and passionate as they devoured each other, discovering how much they have missed each other. They both sucked in a deep breath the moment they parted their lips. At that moment, they found that the bond they shared was more robust than they imagined.

"I love you so much." Loretta's melodious voice hovered over his ears.

"I love you more, honey."

Ray filled two glasses with the pineapple juice. "Honey, let's make a toast."

"To love," Loretta said, her face peaceful.

"To happiness," Ray said. They clicked both glasses and gulped down their drinks. He pulled her close, and she rested her head on his chest. He held her hand in his, feeling her heartbeat.

THE END

Thank you for reading Ties That Bind. Please leave a review on the site of purchase.

ABOUT THE AUTHOR

Stanley Umezulike is an award-winning Nigerian author born in Enugu and raised in Anambra, Nigeria. He is the founder of Prolific Fiction Writers Community on Facebook, where he helps fiction writers gain clarity and learn the art of storytelling.

Stanley writes crime fiction, family drama, and romance set in tropical Africa. He is a graduate of Political Science from the University of Nigeria, Nsukka and did his Master's in International Relations at the same University. He found his passion for writing at the age of 14 and he's been writing ever since. His writing has appeared in various publications including Daily Sun (Nigeria), Creative Freelance Writerz-Africa, and Spillwords.

He is currently working on his next book. Apart from reading and writing, he enjoys watching thriller TV shows, listening to good music and travelling to new places. He lives in Awka, Nigeria. Stanley loves to hear from readers, so follow or drop him a note on Instagram @stanley_umezulike, Twitter @stanumezulike and Facebook at Stanley Umezulike, Author.

Continue reading for a sample from the domestic suspense novel, *__Twisted__* by Stanley Umezilike.

BLURB

The fate of a family hangs in the balance.

The Obi family live a charmed life, the picture of success and love. But when their only son Emeka marries a woman his parents deem unworthy, the ties that bind begin to unravel.

Wealthy, happy and successful, Emeka's world changes when he sets his eyes on Anita, a beautiful teacher who captures his heart. Though his family disapproves, Emeka is determined to make her his wife. But after what was supposed to be a brief introductory ceremony, his perfect world begins to collapse around him.

Determined to build a happy life with his new bride, Emeka keeps his family at a distance. But he soon finds himself immersed in desperate schemes of his overbearing parents, which gets out of hand when he uncovers a secret that threatens to tear the family apart.

Now, the Obi family members are in danger of losing everything they hold dear. The unimaginable is happening and series of events have already begun to push them into the darkest tunnels of their lives. Will they be able to weather this storm or will they be swept away by the tide?

Chapter One (<u>Twisted</u> by Stanley Umezilike)

Present Day
Port Harcourt
"Honey, we are late."
"I am coming! Give me five minutes."
Emeka Obi smiled. He knew Anita better than any other person in the world. He could imagine her calmly going through the steps necessary to make herself appear elegant and presentable. That meant waiting for at least another ten minutes, and possibly more, before she was satisfied with her appearance. Women could waste a lot of time getting dressed.

He was not bothered. He would wait. He put on his black jacket and stepped out of the balcony of his two-storey mansion. At the age of thirty, he looked charming and fit; the perfect picture of the most eligible bachelor, his black afro hair neatly combed. Emeka was of average height, dark-complexioned, with flawless facial features. His artfully carved beard gave him an aristocratic appearance.

The early morning Saturday sun shone directly on his face. He walked faster to his car. His gate man, Yusuf, approached him and collected his briefcase to put in the car trunk. Emeka greeted him with a smile, showcasing his perfect set of white teeth.

"Aaaah."

The sound came from a young man in his late twenties, well past average height. Bob yawned as he walked out of the house. The November sun lunged at his face with its furious rays, making him to blink several times. Television weather forecasters were already saying that this year's cold spell would be longer than usual, with lower temperatures. As his master's driver, Bob was always ready to drive him to his destination. He was already dressed up, but sleep still lingered in his eyes. He approached his master.

"Which car are we using today, sir?"

Emeka had high taste for cars, with six vehicles in different corners around the huge compound—a black Cadillac jeep, a white 2015 Range Rover Sport, a Mercedes-Benz Gle SUV, a blue Infiniti Jeep, a red Lamborghini Aventador, and a black IVM innoson-G5 SUV. The whole compound was paved with marble, with a canopy of well-carved flowers situated at the centre to supply fresh air and add to the beauty of the villa.

"Don't worry, Bob. Yusuf has already opened the Cadillac."

Bob nodded and collected the car key from his boss. Emeka smiled. He looked powerfully built in his long, blue Ankara shirt and trousers. As the only child of his middle class parents who had both suffered to raise him up, his life journey had been tough. His father was now a retired secondary school principal, his mother a consultant nurse working in a private clinic at Enugu. She, too, had long retired from the government civil service.

There had been difficult times when his parents had had no money to pay for his school fees. Constant strikes by the labour union shrunk the meagre-pay of their government jobs to almost being insufficient. At one point, when Emeka's school fees in the university skyrocketed, his father had almost given up. Somehow, his mother had managed to pay them so that he could remain in school. Back then, she'd been a senior nurse working at the university teaching hospital at Enugu.

After graduating with a degree in civil engineering from the University of Nigeria, Nsukka, Emeka had worked with a lot of construction companies before opening his own business. His father had proudly helped him to secure a loan from a micro-finance bank.

Now, almost everywhere he looked, he could see the result of his parents' efforts in shaping his life. Emeka had started building a network of connections, welcoming new friendships. With his charming eyes and permanent smile, he was very persuasive and likable. To him, he felt his special gift had more to do with talent than effort.

His major breakthrough came when he secured a government contract to reconstruct the East-West Road. From then, it had been one success after another. At the age of twenty-five, he had begun to deal in import and export of building materials. Later that year, he'd opened his own paint manufacturing company.

Since then, he had been acquiring failing companies. He would buy them and refit them with experts, and before long, they would start generating money. The next thing he did was acquire a big advertising agency. He spent millions in advertising, and he generated even more profit.

Three years later, *Emeka and Sons Group of Companies* finally became a publicly traded company registered on the Nigerian Stock Exchange. Now, it had become a big corporation with shareholders and board of directors, and at the head of this giant sat Emeka, the Chief Executive Officer.

His parents had been worried that he had shunned the idea of marriage. They'd accused him of refusing to marry. For the past seven years, Emeka had focused on his business—from one acquisition to another, from one deal to another. As if he were driving an unstoppable train ... it had to stop temporary when he set his eyes on Anita, who eventually turned out to be the beautiful queen of his heart.

Today, he was travelling to Enugu with his fiancée to introduce her to his parents.

The sound of the horn interrupted his thoughts. He looked up and met her eyes. Anita looked beautiful in her blue Ankara gown. She was a tall, ebony beauty, an inch taller than him. Her eyes were filled with love as she smiled at him.

Emeka approached her, kissed her right hand, and led her to the car. They entered through the back door, and Bob drove the car out of the compound.

Their beautiful mansion was located at Peter Odili Road—a place reserved for the wealthy, part of the Trans Amadi industrial district and a few kilometres away from the Port Harcourt city centre. Port Harcourt, the city that never sleeps, was the capital of the oil-rich Rivers State. Romantics often referred to it as the 'Garden City' because of its flowery avenues and beautiful ornaments.

In less than thirty minutes, they were driving through Rumuola Road, known for its notorious traffic jam. Though still around nine in the morning, the heavy traffic slowed down their journey.

Rivers State government should do something about this hold-up.

Twenty minutes later, they were driving through Aba-Port-Harcourt expressway. They reached Enugu around one in the afternoon.

Located in South-Eastern Nigeria with a population of more than two million, Enugu actually meant 'Hill top,' denoting the city's hilly geography. But yet, Enugu lay at the foot of an escarpment and not a hill. Known as the coal city, it was popular for its cool and serene environment and the coal mineral it had in abundance.

"Are we almost there?" Anita asked anxiously.

Emeka held her hand.

"Yes, get ready. Don't worry, you will be fine. I'm with you," he assured her.

Anita was panicking. A lot of things had been going on in her mind. Today was like a judgment day. *Will they like me? What will they say?*

A lot of questions were flowing through her mind, but only two things helped to calm her down and give her confidence: the love of her life sitting beside her, and the diamond ring on her finger.

She placed her hand with the ring on her chest and muttered silent prayers.

***

Trans-Ekulu, Enugu

"They will soon be here," she said.

"Yes, finally, a woman has captured his heart. I can't wait to see her," he said.

Rita Obi and her husband, Sir Matthew Obi, held hands together as they stepped out of the door of their gorgeous one-storey duplex. Emeka had bought the land at Trans-Ekulu housing estate and built the duplex for them, tastefully furnishing it to their taste. Beautiful trees and shrubs helped to give the compound exactly what they wanted—a quiet, peaceful atmosphere.

Known to her friends as the 'Diamond Butterfly', Rita Obi was a tall, mahogany-skinned woman with an imposing stature and a variable temperament; she could be very gentle and tender one moment, and roaring like a lioness the next. Her husband often joked that not only could she bite ... she could bite very hard.

Because of her imposing physique, a lot of people who knew her now believed that nurses were wicked. But Rita knew she was not wicked. In a man's world, a woman must either keep the men under her feet to gain their respect and admiration, or they would put her under their feet to serve as their tools and properties. She had been eating a lot of food lately, and her curvy, plump frame had made her maids in the house so fearful of her.

Sir Matthew Obi was exactly the opposite of his wife. To maintain balance in a family, there should always be the iron rod and the tender hand. He was the tender hand. A member of the Catholic Knights of St John, he was gentle but firm. Highly conservative and fair-skinned, he was a man of principles and a little above average height, five years older than his wife. At the age of sixty-five, the retired school principal was still ruggedly handsome with flecks of grey hair. He looked up as he heard the sound of a car horn.

"They are here," he said as he smiled.

An elderly gateman opened the gate, and the Cadillac jeep cruised into the compound and stopped in front of the house.

"Stay in the car," Emeka told Bob as he led his fiancée out of the vehicle.

Anita's face beamed as her gown sparkled under the afternoon sun. Emeka maintained a smile on his face as he approached his parents. He had always been very close to his mother—he loved her so much. Since his childhood, her hands had left their marks in virtually every stage of his life. He hugged her tightly.

"Welcome, my son," Rita said as her face lit up in a smile showing her white teeth.

Emeka shook hands with his father. Sir Matthew Obi turned and greeted the young girl.

"Welcome, Nne."

Anita greeted back politely.

Emeka quickly introduced them. "Mama, Papa, this is Anita, the love of my life."

Rita scanned the young woman's face for a long moment, her heavy gaze was intense, making Anita feel uncomfortable.

Quickly, a smile crept back to her face. "Finally. So you are the one. Come and give me a hug."

Anita's discomfort quickly faded, and she became so excited. *What a warm welcome. I can't wait to be a member of this lovely family.* She hugged her future mother-in-law in an earnest embrace, and they entered the house. Soon, they were climbing the tiled stairs. On their way up, she looked down stairs and saw two young teenage girls, probably maids. They were busy hurrying up and down, putting things in order.

At the dining room, expensive plates had already been set on the enormous mahogany round table. They were all served African salad with beef by one of the maids. The second course was pounded yam and vegetable soup with fresh fish, this one carefully served by Emeka's mother.

As Anita observed the way Emeka was enjoying the pounded yam, she made a mental note to add it as one of his favourite foods. The whole family was so adorable. Father and mother sat close to each other as they ate and looked at their only son with eyes filled with love. The son sat facing his parents as he looked at them with eyes filled with devotion. Their faces all beamed with smiles as they cracked small jokes and laughed tenderly.

She was touched by the memorable moment she was witnessing. She wished she had parents like this. Everything was so perfect. Sometimes, the mother would feed the father and help him with a glass of water, and they would all smile. She was looking at a happy family with their golden son at the centre of their universe.

"Nne, which town are you from?" Matthew asked.

Emeka looked on as his fiancée answered. He had already finished eating. His mother was helping him with a bowl of water to wash his hands.

"I am a native of Ikwerre in Rivers State."

"That's wonderful," Matthew exclaimed. "I worked there during my NYSC service year. Some of my friends are from your town. They are all wonderful. Ikwerre people are very welcoming and friendly. They made me feel at home. We are delighted to have you in our midst. You are highly welcome."

Anita blushed. "Thank you, sir."

Before long, they started throwing questions after questions at her, and she kept responding politely.

"When did you meet our son?" This question was asked by Emeka's mother.

Surprised, Anita maintained her smile and answered. "Last year, ma'am."

"Hmmm." Rita looked at her with a renewed interest. "That was when our son was already a ready-made man. When our son was struggling, trying to put his two feet on the ground, no woman wanted anything to do with him."

She paused for a moment, a thoughtful expression was on her face. "Nne, can you say that what attracted you to our son was not his money?"

Anita was overwhelmed by the sudden turn of events. "No, Ma. We met and we fell in love."

There was a crack of laughter.

"Really? That's a unique love story. All in less than a year," Rita said.

Emeka was getting uncomfortable now.

"How long have you been in the city?" Matthew asked.

"I was born and brought up in the city," Anita replied.

"In other words, you grew up in the city ..." Rita left her statement hanging.

"Yes, Ma." Anita was now uncomfortable.

"Hmm. Our son is lucky to have found himself a city girl," Rita muttered quietly. "How many relationships have you been involved in before meeting our son?"

Anita's eyes widened. Emeka quickly wiped the sweat off his forehead and put the handkerchief back inside his pocket. Then, he stopped every other thing he was doing.

Before Anita could answer the question, his mother hurled another question at her.

"Have you known a man before meeting our son?"

"What?" Anita asked in bewilderment.

Emeka's blood boiled with every coming second. His breath had quickened, his mind trying to make sense of the sudden turn of events.

This is madness.

Rita smiled. "Who are you playing pastor's daughter for? Loose it down, young lady. Don't be all innocent on me."

"Enough!" Emeka shouted as he stood up. "What is happening here? This is uncalled for," he said as his parents stared at him, surprised.

"Go to the car. Wait for me. We are leaving now," he whispered in Anita's ear.

"But—"

"Go!"

Anita rose up, fidgeting, and walked slowly out of the house.

"What is this? An interrogation?"

"Don't shout at your mother, Emeka," his father warned.

He glared at his parents and began to walk out of the dining room.

"Emeka!"

His mother's voice always had a way of getting to him. He stopped in his tracks and looked back.

"We have decided," she announced.

"Decided what?" he inquired angrily.

"Emeka, we are your parents. We want what is best for you and our family. You will not marry that girl into this family," his father ordered.

Emeka was highly baffled at his father's words. He had been so happy when he had seen Anita.

Mother!

She had somehow imposed her decisions on father again.

"Anya ya emepego. Her eyes have opened," his mother said. "She is a gold digger."

This was the last straw that broke the camel's back. Emeka turned back and stormed out of the house.

"Darling, I don't understand. What is happening?" Anita asked as he joined her in the car.

"She has done it again, but I won't allow it this time," he said.

"What? Who?"

He ignored her, not in the mood to answer any more questions. "Bob, start this car and drive us out of here."

Bob started the car and drove it towards the exit. The elderly gateman opened the gate, and their car sped off into the hot afternoon sun. What started as a perfect day had turned into a nightmare.

OTHER BOOKS BY LOVE AFRICA PRESS

Beautiful Mess by Mukami Ngari
Betting On Love by Kani Sey
Scar's Redemption by Kiru Taye
The Torn Prince by Zee Monodee

CONNECT WITH US

Facebook.com/LoveAfricaPress
Twitter.com/LoveAfricaPress
Instagram.com/LoveAfricaPress

SIGN UP TO OUR NEWSLETTER
https://www.loveafricapress.com/newsletter

www.ingramcontent.com/pod-product-compliance
Lightning Source LLC
Chambersburg PA
CBHW020758190726
48285CB00006B/2087